Fridthjof's Saga

Esaias Tegnér

Contents

FRIDTHJOF'S SAGA

BY

Esaias Tegne'r

NOTE BY THE TRANSLATORS

Tegne'r's poem, "Fridthjof's Saga," has been printed in Sweden in many large editions and in almost every possible style. It has been illustrated, and it has been set to music. It has been translated into nearly all the modern European languages. Moreover it has been rendered into English by eighteen different translators, and has been twice reprinted in America. Bayard Taylor edited an American edition of a translation by Rev. William L. Blackley of Dublin, and published it about ten years ago. Professor R. B. Anderson has just published in his "Viking Tales," a translation made by Professor George Stephens of Copenhagen, and which received the sanction of Bishop Tegne'r himself.

And yet we venture to add another, and present here the first complete American translation. Mr. Taylor said in his preface to Blackley's version that there had never been an English Fridthjof's Saga which was satisfactory to Swedes. This is probably owing to the fact that the Swedes have become so familiar with its original measures and so accustomed to its peculiar rhythm, that they cannot willingly dispense with any part of the form which Tegne'r gave it. Several of the metres employed by him were unknown to Swedish readers
until they appeared in this poem. Tegne'r's experiment of introducing them was
a successful one; and they are now, in the minds of Swedes, as much a part of the work as the story itself. The feminine rhymes, occurring in fifteen of the twenty-four cantos, are so melodious that no one who had heard the original,

even if he did not understand a word of it, could be quite satisfied with a version which does not reproduce them. The feminine rhymes and the alliteration of Canto XXI have presented obstacles which no single translation has hitherto overcome.

The original measures the feminine rhymes and the alliteration of "Ring's Drapa," are, in our estimation, essential features of a good rendering of the poem, and if we have done our work well we do not fear that any one will think there are too many translations.

For a fuller history of "Fridthjof 's Saga" than can be given in this note, we refer the reader to Anderson's "Viking Tales," where the sagas on which this story is founded appear in full.

The preparation of this translation has been a home work which has brightened for us the firelight of many a pleasant evening. We publish it in full faith that it will have a like happy effect in whatever home it may be read.

October, 1876.

CHARACTERS

Bele. (Pronounced Bay'-lay.) King of Sogn, in Norway.

Helge (Hel'-gay) and Halfdan. His sons.

Ingeborg. (Ing'-e-borg.) His daughter.

Thorstein. (Tor'-stine.) A peasant, -friend and companion-in-arms of King Bele.

Fridthjof. (Freet'-yof.) Son of Thorstein.

Hilding. Foster-father and teacher of Fridthjof and Ingeborg.

Bjorn. (B'yorn.) A sworn foster-brother of Fridthjof.

Ring. King of Ringric, in Norway.

Angantyr. (Ang'-an-teer.) Ruler of the Orkney Islands.

Atle. (At'-lay.) A berserk, and one orf Angantyr's warriors.

SCENE--Northern Norway and the Orkney Islands.

Fridthjof and Ingeborg.

In Hilding's garden, green and fair,
Protected by his fostering care,
Two rare and stately plants were growing,
Unequaled grace and beauty showing.

The one a sturdy oak tree grew,
With lance-like stem so straight and true,
Its crown in northern tempests shaking
Like helmet plume in battle quaking.

The other like a rose sprang forth
When tardy winter leaves the north,
And spring, which in the buds lies dreaming,
Still waits with gems to set them gleaming.

Around the earth the storm-king raves,
The wrestling oak its anger braves;
The sun dissolves frost's mantle hoary,
The buds reveal their hidden glory.

So they grew up in joy and glee,
And Fridthjof was the young oak tree;
Unfolding in the vale serenely,
The rose was Ingeborg the queenly.

Saw you those two by light of day
You seem in Freyja's house to stay,
Where bride-pairs, golden-haired, were swinging,
Their way on rosy pinions winging.

But seeing them by moonlight pale
Round dancing in the leafy vale,
You'd think: The elf-king now advances,
And leads his queen in fairy dances.

How joyful 'twas, how lovely too,
When firs[he learned his futhorc through;
No kings had e'er such honor brought them
As when to Ingeborg he taught them.

How joyously his boat would glide
With those two o'er the dark blue tide:
While he the driving sail was veering,
Her small white hands gave hearty cheering.

No bird's nest found so high a spot,
That he for her could find it not;
The eagle's nest from clouds he sundered,
And eggs and young he deftly plundered.

However swift, there ran no brook,
But o'er it Ingeborg he took;
How sweet when roaring torrents frighten,
To feel her soft arms round him tighten.
The first; spring flowers by sunshine fed,
The earliest berries turning red,
The first of autumn's golden treasure,
He proffered her with eager pleasure.

****

But quickly sped are childhood's days,--
There stands a youth whose ardent gaze
With pleading and with hope is laden,
And there, with budding charms, a maiden.

Young Fridthjof followed oft the chase,
Which led to many a fearful place;
With neither spear nor lance defended,
The wild bear's life he quickly ended.

When, struggling, met they breast to breast,
The hunter won, though hardly pressed,
And brought the bearskin home; such prizes,
Think you, a maiden e'er despises?

For woman values courage rare;
The brave alone deserves the fair,
Each one the other's grace completing,
As brow and helmet fitly meeting.

And when in winter evenings long,
By firelight reading, in a song,
Of fair abodes in radiant heaven

To every god and goddess given,

He thought: "Of gold is Ing'borg's hair,
A net for rose and lily fair:
Like Freyja's bounteous golden tresses,
A wheat-field which the breeze caresses.

Fair Idun's beauteous bosom beats
Beneath the green silk's safe retreats,--
I know a silk whose sheen encloses
Light; fairies two, with buds of roses.

And Frigg's mild eyes are blue and clear
As heaven, when no clouds appear,--
But I know eyes beside whose sparkles
A light, blue spring day quickly darkles.

And Gerd's fair cheeks, why praise them so?
The northern-lights, on new fall'n snow,--
I know of cheeks whose rosy warnings
Portray at once two ruddy mornings.

I know a heart affection-crowned
Like Nanna's, though not so renowned
And Nanna's love, in song and story,
is justly reckoned Balder's glory.

For oh, what joy when death appears,
To have a faithful maiden's tears!
To prove a love so strong and tender,
With Hel's grim shades I'd gladly wander."

Meanwhile the princess gayly wove
In cloth, blue wave and greenest grove;
And as she sang a hero's story,
She also wove a hero's glory.

For soon there grew in snow-white wool
Bright shields from off the golden spool,
Here, red prevail the battle lances,

There, silver-stiffened armor glances.

Anon her fingers deftly trace
A hero,--see, 'tis Fridthjof's face;
And though at first almost affrighted,
She blushes, smiles and is delighted.

The birch tree's stem where Fridthjof went
Showed I and F in beauty blent;
As grew those runes in one, delighted,
So too those hearts in one united.

When Day invests the upper air,
The world-king with the golden hair,
When men to action urge each other,
They think alone of one another.

When Night pervades the upper air,
The world-queen with the raven hair,
When stars in silence greet each other,
They dream alone of one another.

"Thou Earth, who in the spring-time fair,
Bedeck'st with flowers thine emerald hair,
Give me the best; in wreaths I'll wind them,
And round my Fridthjof's brow will bind them."

"Thou sea, who mak'st thy dark caves bright
With myriad pearls' refulgent light,
Give me the best; I'll weave the clearest
A necklace for my Ing'borg dearest."

"Thou ornament of Odin's throne,
Eye of the world, O golden sun,
Wert thou but mine, thy blazing splendor
I'd give a shield to my defender."

"Thou guide in Odin's house at night,
Thou pale moon with thy lovely light,
Were thou but mine, thy pearly lustre
'Mid Ing'borg's golden hair should cluster."

But Hilding said: "My foster-son,
Your reason is by love outrun;
The norns are partial in bestowing
The blood that in her veins is flowing.

To Odin high, where bright stars shine,
Ascendeth her ancestral line;
No hope may son of Thorstein nourish,
For like with like alone can flourish."

But Fridthjof smiled: "My race," he said,
"Goes down unto the valiant dead;
The forest-king I slew, and merit
Thereby, the honor kings inherit.

"The free-born man will never yield,
He owns the world's unconquered field;
For fate can bind what she has broken,
And hope is crowned with kingly token.

"All power is noble; Thor presides
In Thrudvang, where all strength abides;

There worth, and not descent, is leader,--
The sword is e'er a valiant pleader.

"I'd fight the world for my sweet bride,
Yea, though the thunder-god defied.
Be glad and brave, my lily, never
Shah mortal dare our lives to sever."

II.
King Bele And Thorstein.

King Bele, sword-supported, in the palace stood;
And with him Thorstein, Viking's son, the peasant good.
His ancient war companion, grown old in glory,
His brow was scarred like rune-stones, his hair was hoary.

They stood, as on the mountain two temples stand
To honored gods devoted, now half in sand;
And many words of wisdom the walls are saying,
And holy recollections through domes are straying.

"The evening steals upon me," king Bele said,
"The helmet now is heavy, and stale the mead;
The fate of man grows darker, but all the clearer
High Valhal shines before me, as death draws nearer.

"My sons I here have summoned, and Thorstein's son
For they should cling together, as we have done;
But I would give the eaglets some words of warning--
Words may in death be sleeping ere dawns the morning."

Obedient to the mandate, the three advance--
First, Helge, dark and gloomy, with sullen glance;
He dwelt amid diviners; the hand he proffered

Was red with blood of victims, on altars offered.

The next who came was Halfdan, a light-haired swain:
His countenance was noble, but weak and vain;
He gaily bore a falchion, with which he gestured,
And seemed a youthful maiden, in armor vestured.

And after them came Fridthjof, in mantle blue;
He was stronger than the others, and taller, too;
He stood between the brothers, by contrast seeming
Like noon 'twixt night and morning, in splendor beaming.

"Ye sons," the king said gently, "my son goes down;
Together rule the kingdom and take the crown;
For unity is power, and no endeavor,
While lance with ring is circled, its stem can sever.

"Let power stand as sentry on every hand,
And freedom bloom protected throughout the land:
The sword is for protection, and not for plunder.
And shields are locks for peasants no foe can sunder.

"How foolish is the ruler his land to oppress,
For the people give the power which kings possess;
The crown of leafy verdure which decks the mountain
Will wither if the sunshine dries up the fountain.

"On four gigantic pillars is heaven's throne--
The throne of nations resteth on law alone!
Destruction waits on judgment; if misdirected;
By right are men ennobled and kings perfected.

"In Disarsal, O Helge, the high gods dwell--
Not pinioned as the snail is within his shell;
As far as daylight flieth, or thought's swift pinion,
Far as resound the echoes, is gods' dominion.

The offered hawk gives tokens which oft deceive.
Not all runes monumental can we believe:
But an honest heart, O Helge, of pure endeavor,
With Odin's runes is written, misleading never.

"Be not severe, king Helge, but firm and staid;
The sword that bites the sharpest has the limberest blade.
Kings are adorned by mercy, as shields by flowers,
And spring can more accomplish than winter's powers.

"A man, however mighty, deprived of friends,
Like tree of bark denuded, how soon life ends!
But he by friends surrounded, like trees shall flourish,
Whose crowns, in groves protected, the brooklets nourish.

"Boast not ancestral wisdom; each man alone
A single bowstring uses, and that his own;
What matters it to any the worth that's buried?
By its own waves the current o'er seas is carried.

"A joyous spirit, Halfdan, advantage brings,
But idle talk is needless, and most, to kings;
Of hops, as well as honey, is mead compounded,
Let sports on vigor, lances on steel, be founded.

"No man has too much wisdom, though learned he be,
And much too little, many less learned than he;
To fools, though high in station, no praise is meted,

The wise hy all are honored, though lowly seated.

"The steadfast friend, O Halfdan! of mingled blood,
Lives near indeed, though distant be his abode;
But to thy foeman's dwelling the way is weary,--
Though standing by thy pathway, 'tis far and dreary.

"For friend choose not the first one that's so disposed,--
An empty house stands open, a full one closed;
Choose one, the best, O Halfdan, nor seek another,
The world soon knows the secrets of three together."

These words then Thorstein uttered in clearest tone:
"King Bele unto Odin goes not alone;
We've always stood together, whatever tried us,
And death, now drawing near, shall not divide us.

"Fridthjof, old age hath whispered in my rapt ear
Full many words of wisdom, which thou must hear.
Birds fly from graves to Odin, with wisdom freighted,
The words by old men spoken, should not be slighted.

"First, give the high gods honor; for good or ill,
Storms come as well as sunshine, by Heaven's will.
The gods perceive the secrets in thy possession.
And years must make atonement for each transgression.

"Obey the king: most wisely rules one alone,
The eyes of night are many, day has but one.
The better are contented by best directed,--
The blade must have a handle to be perfected.

Great strength is heaven's dower; but, Fridthjof, learn
That power devoid of wisdom, can little earn.
Strong bears by one are taken,--one man of reason;
Set shields to turn the sword stroke, let law stop treason.

"A few may fear the haughty, whom all despise,
And with the proud in spirit, destruction lies:
Those once flew high, who're now on crutches creeping;
The winds rule fortune, weather, time of reaping.

"The day thou'lt rightly prize, whose sun has sunk,
Advice when it is followed, and ale when drunk.
The hopes of youth on shadows are often rested,
But strength of sword and friendship, by use are 'tested.

"Trust not the snow of spring-time, nor night-old ice;
The serpent when he sleepeth, nor girl's advice;
The mind of changeful woman not long abideth,
And fickleness of spirit, 'neath flower-tints hideth.

"All men will surely perish with all they prize,
But one thing know I, Fridthjof, which never dies,--
And that is reputation', therefore, ever
The noble action strive for, the good endeavor."

So warned the aged chieftains in the palace hall.
As since the skald has chanted in Ha'vama'l,
So passed these sayings pithy through generations;
And still from graves they whisper 'mid northern nations.

Then many words and heartfelt, these warriors found
To tell their lasting friendship, so wide renowned.
How friends till death, if fortune or frowned or slighted.

Like two hands clasped together they stood united.

"And back to back in battle we held the field,
And which way norns did threaten, they smote a shield;
Before you now to Valhal we old men hasten,
And may their fathers' spirit our children's chasten."

The king said much concerning brave Fridthjof's worth,
Heroic power surpassing all royal birth;
And much was said by Thorstein, how graces cluster
Round Northland's honored monarchs, with Asa-lustre.

"But hold ye fast together, ye children three,
The Northland then your conqueror shall never see;
For royalty and power, when duly ordered,
Are like a bright shield golden, by blue steel bordered.

"Salute my daughter Ing'borg, the rosebud sweet,
In quiet was she nurtured, as seemed meet:
Protect her, lest the storm-king, with cruel power,
Should fasten in his helmet my tender flower.

"I lay on thee, king Helge, a father's care,
Love Ing'borg as a daughter, the jewel rare!
Restraint galls noble spirits, but gentle manner
Will lead both man and woman to right and honor.

"But lay us now, ye children, in two mound-graves.
Close where the blue gulf tosses its ceaseless waves;
Our souls shall then forever enjoy the ringing
Of dirges which in breaking the waves are singing.

"When the moon's pale beams the mountains and valleys fill,
And midnight's dew is falling on grove and hill;
Then will we sit, O Thorstein, above our pillows,
And talk about the future, across the billows.

"And now, farewell, ye children, our work is done;
Unto the Allfather gladly we hasten on,
Like weary rivers longing for sea's caressing;
On you be Thor's and Odin's and Frey's rich blessing."

III

Buried were Bele and Thorstein together, as they had commanded;
High rose their grave-mounds on each side the gulf by the blue rolling water,
Death having sundered the hearts that in life were so closely united.
Helge and Halfdan, by will of the people, took jointly the kingdom
Left by their father; but Fridthjof, an only son, heired alone Framness,
Took unmolested possession, and settled himself there in quiet.

Stretching around him for twelve miles unbroken his acres extended;
Three sides were dale, hill and mountain, the fourth side looked out on the ocean;
Crowned were the hill-tops with forests of birch-wood, but, on their sides sloping,
Golden corn plentiful grew, and like billows the tall rye was waving.
Many in number the lakes which their mirrors held up for the mountains;
Held them up, too, for the woods in whose thickets the high-horned elks wandered,
Making there kingly roads, drinking from running brooks counted by hundreds.
But in the valleys wide, on the smooth greensward were quietly grazing
Glossy-skinned herds, which with udders distended now long for the milk-pail.
Scattered among them were myriads of white-wooled sheep, constantly moving,
Looking like fleecy clouds sailing serenely across the blue heavens,

Wafted now hither now thither in crowds by the winds in the spring-time.

Twelve times two coursers, fierce whirlwinds, defiant though fettered,
Stood in the rows of stalls, stamping and restless, the meadow-hay chewing,
Knotted their long manes with red, and their hoofs were with iron shoes glistening.

Standing apart was the drinking-hall, built of the choicest fir timber;
Counting ten twelves to the hundred, not five hundred warriors assembled
Filled up the spacious apartment, when all met to drink mead at Yule-time.
Down through the middle, from end to end, ran a strong table of stone-oak,
Polished with wax and like steel shining; carved on two pillars of elm-wood,
Far at one end, Frey and Odin supported the dais of honor,
Odin with lordly look, Frey with the sun for a crest on his bonnet.

'Twixt the two, on a bear-skin (black as a coal was this bear-skin,
Scarlet the mouth, while the tips of the claws were with bright silver shining),
Thorstein among his friends sat--hospitality ministering to Gladness.

Oft when the moon in the heavens was riding, the old man related
Wonders of foreign lands seen by him when as a viking he journeyed,
Far on the waves of the Baltic, the White, and the Northern seas tossing.
Mutely the company listened. Fixed were their eyes on the speaker,
Even as bees upon roses; the poet was thinking of Brage,[1]

Brage with silver beard flowing, and tongue clothed in wisdom the choicest,
Sitting 'neath shadowy birches, telling a story by Mimer's
Unceasingly murmuring fountain, he too a saga unending.
Covered with straw was the floor, and upon a walled hearth in the center,

---

1   Bra'-gay

Constantly burned, warm and cheerful, a fire, while down the wide chimney
Twinkling stars, heavenly friends, glanced upon guest and hall, quite
unforbidden.

Studded with nails were the walls, and upon them were hanging
Helmets and coats-of-mail closely together; also between them
Here and there flashed down a sword, like a meteor shooting at evening.
Brighter than helmet or sword were the sparkling shields ranged round the
chamber;
Bright as the time of the sun were they, clear as the moon's disc of silver.
Oft as the horns needed filling, there passed round the table a maiden;
Modestly blushing she cast down her eyes, her beautiful image
Mirrored appeared in the shields, and gladdened the heart of each warrior.

Rich was the house, and the eye of the stranger, whichever way gazing,
Rested on cellar well filled, or on pantry or press overflowing.
Jewels the rarest, trophies of conquest, gleamed in profusion;
Gold carved in runes with great skill, and wonderful things wrought in silver.
Chief in this limitless treasure three things were most of all valued.

First of the three was a sword, which from sire and from grandsire descended.
Called Angervadil, or grief-wader, sometimes, too, brother of lightning.
Far, far away in the East it was forged--so at least says the story--
Tempered in fire by the dwarfs. Bjorn Bluetooth the first one who bore it.

Bjorn lost at once both the sword and his life in a bravely-fought battle,
Southward in Groning Sound, where he struggled with Vifil the powerful.
Vifil's possessions descended to Viking.

    At Woolen-Acre,
Old and infirm, there lived a great king with a beautiful daughter.
See, from the depths of the forest there cometh a giant misshapen,
Higher in stature than man, a monster ferocious and shaggy,

Boldly demanding a hand-to-hand combat, or kingdom and daughter.

No one, however, accepted the challenge, for none had a weapon
Able his hard skull to pierce, and therefore they called him the Iron-skull.

Viking, whose winters scarce fifteen had numbered, nobly advancing,
Entered the fray, secure in his strong arm and good Angervadil.
Cleft at one blow the hideous goblin, and rescued the maiden.
Viking bequeathed the good weapon to Thorstein, his son, and Thorstein,
To Odin ascended, bequeathed it to Fridthjof. Whenever he drew it,
Light filled the hall as when northern lights entered, or lightning flashed
through it.
Hammered of gold was the hilt, with strange letters 'twas covered;
Wonderful mysteries were they in Northland, but known to the people
Who dwell near the gates of the sun, where our fathers lived ere they came
hither.

Faint were the runes when the land was in quiet throughout all its borders;
But when the followers of Hild were summoned, then were they burning
Red as the comb of a cock when he fighteth. Lost was the warrior
Who met, on the field of encounter, the blade with its red letters glowing.
Highly renowned was that sword, and of swords was the chief in the North-
land.

Next highly prized was the ponderous arm-ring, widely notorious,
Forged by the Vulcan of northern tradition, the halting smith Volund;
Three marks it weighed, and gold was the metal of which it was fashioned;
Carved were the heavens with twelve towering castles, where dwell the
immortals,--
Emblem of changing months, called by the poets the sun's glorious dwelling.
First there was Frey's castle Alfheim, that is the sun, which born newly,
Starts once again to ascend the steep pathway of Heaven at Yule-time.
There too was Sokvabek; seated within it were Odin and Saga

Drinking together their wine from a gold shell,--that shell is the Ocean,
Colored with gold from the glow of the morning. Saga is Spring-time,
Writ on the green of the fresh springing field, with flowers for letters.
Balder, the kingly, is pictured there, throned on the sun at midsummer,
Which pours from the firmament riches untold,-- personified goodness;
For lights are the good, radiant, resplendent, but the evil are darkness.
Constantly rising the sun groweth weary; the good also falter,
Giddy with walking precipitous heights; sighing they downward
Sink to the land of the shades,--down to Hel. That is of Balder
The funeral pile. Glitner, the castle of Peace, is there; seated
Within it was Forse'te',[2] scales in hand, meting out justice.

Many more pictures with these there engraven, betoken the conflict
Waged against darkness, on earth and in heaven; bright were they shining,
Wrought by a master's hand on the broad arm-ring. Clustering rubies
Crown its high center, e'en as in summer the sun crowns the heavens.
Long was the circlet a family heir-loom. On the side of the mother
Traced they their pedigree back to old Volund, ancestor mighty.
Once, says tradition, the jewel was stolen by robber named Soti,
Roaming abroad through the seas. Long was it ere 'twas recovered.
Finally (so runs the story) 'twas said that the robber had buried
Himself with his ship, and. his treasure, deep on the far coast of Britain.
Pleasure or quiet he found not, a ghost was his irksome companion.
Hearing the rumor, Thorstein with Bele the dragon ship mounted,
Dashed through the foaming waves, straight to the place of the sepulcher
steering.
Wide as a temple's arch, or a king's gateway, bedded in gravel,
Covered with grassy turf, arched to the top, the tomb rose forbidding.
Light issued from it. Through a small crevice within the closed portal,
Peered the two champions. There the pitched viking ship
Stood with its masts, its yards and its anchor. High in the stern sheets
Was seated a terrible figure, clad in a mantle all flaming,

2　For-se-te

Furious demon scouring a blade that with blood spots was covered.
Vain was his labor, naught could remove them. All his rich booty
Round him was scattered, and on his arm was the ring he had stolen.

"Go we," said Bele, "down thither and fight with the hideous goblin,
Two 'gainst a spirit of fire." But Thorstein half angrily answered:
"One against one is the rule of our fathers. I fight well singly."
Long they contended which first of the two the encounter should venture,
Proving the perilous journey. Bele at last took his helmet,
Shaking two lots therein. Watched by the stars Thorstein saw by their shimmer
His was the lot first appearing. A blow from his javelin of iron
Cleft the huge bolts and strong locks. He descended. Did any one question
What was revealed in the cavern, then was he silent and shuddered.
Bele at first heard strange music. It rang like the song of a goblin;
Then was a clattering noise, like the clashing of blades in a combat,
Lastly a hideous shriek,--then silence. Out staggered Thorstein,
Confounded, bewildered, all pale was his face, for with death had he battled;
Yet bore he the arm-ring a trophy. "'Twas dear bought," he often said frowning;
"Once in my life was I frightened; 'twas when I recovered that arm-ring."
Widely renowned was that ring, and of rings was the chief in the Northland.

Lastly the ship, called Ellide, was one of the family jewels.
Viking, so say they, returning triumphant from venturesome journeys,
Sailed along coasting near Framness. There he espied on a shipwreck,
Carelessly swinging, a sailor, sporting as 'twere with the billows.
Noble of figure, tall in his stature, joyful his visage,
Changeable too, like the waves of the sea when they sport ill the sunshine,--
Blue was his mantle, golden his girdle and studded with corals;
Sea-green his hair, but his beard was as white as the foam of the ocean.
Viking his serpent steered thither to rescue the unfortunate stranger,--
Took him half frozen to Framness, and there as a guest entertained him.

When by his host to repose he was bidden, smiling he answered:
"Fair sits the wind, and my ship which you boarded, is not yet disabled;
Long ere the morning I trust she will hear me a hundred miles seaward.
Thanks for thy bidding, 'twas well meant and kindly. Ah! could I only
Leave thee a gift to remind thee of me! but afar on the ocean
Lieth my kingdom. Perhaps in the morning 'twill waft thee a token."
Viking next day by the sea-shore was standing, when lo! like an eagle
Madly pursuing its prey, a dragon ship sailed into harbor.
Nowhere was visible sailor or captain, or even a steersman;
Winding 'mid rocks and through breakers, the rudder a path sought unaided;
When the firm strand it was nearing, sudden, as ruled by a spirit,
Reefed were the sails unassisted. Untouched by finger of mortal,
The anchor sped through the clear water and fastened its barbs in the bottom.
Viking gazed, speechless with wonder; the sportive winds sang in low ca-
dence:
"AEger the rescued forgetteth no kindness, he gives thee the dragon."
Kingly the gift to behold. The heavy curved planks of oak timber
Matched not together like others, but grew in one broad piece united.
It stretched its huge form in the sea like a dragon, its stem proudly lifted,
A stately head high in the air. Its throat with red gold was all blazing;
Sprinkled its belly with yellow and azure, and back of the rudder,
Covered with scales of pure silver, its tail lashed the waves in a circle.
Bordered with red were its inky black pinions. When all unfolding,
It flew in a race with the whirlwind, and left far behind the swift eagle.
When it was filled with armed warriors, you'd fancy you were beholding
A citadel swimming the billows, or palace o'er ocean ave flying.
Widely renowned was that ship, and of ships was the chief in the Northland.

All this and other vast treasures did Fridthjof receive from his father.
Scarce was there found in the Northland any with richer possessions,
Save were he heir of a kingdom, for of kings is the wealth always greatest.
Though from no king he descended, yet was his mind truly royal,
Courteous, noble and kind. Daily became he more famous.

Twelve gray-haired champions, valorous chieftains, sat at his table,
Thorstein's steel-breasted companions, whose brows were with scars deeply
furrowed.
Next to the warriors was seated a youth of the same age as Fridthjof,--

Like a fresh rose 'mid the dry leaves of autumn; Bjorn was this blossom.
Grown up with Fridthjof, in days of their boyhood their blood they commin-
gled,
Brothers becoming in good northern fashion, sworn to each other
In joy and in grief, the survivor avenging the death of his comrade.

In the midst of the warriors and guests who had come to the funeral banquet,
Fridthjof, a sorrowing host, his eyelids with tears overflowing
Drank in accordance with ancestral usage, a skoal to his father,
Heard the old minstrels sing loudly his praises, a thundering drapa,
Rightfully took of his late father's seat undisputed possession,
And sat between Odin and Frey. So sitteth Thor up in Valhal.

IV.
Fridthjof's Courtship.

Loud sounded the music in Fridthjof's hall,
His ancestors' praises sang poets all.
O'erwhelmed with sadness
Is Fridthjof, he hears not their songs of gladness.

The earth has again donned her mantle of green
And dragon-ships breasting the waves are seen
But Fridthjof, pondering,
Is at the moon gazing or in the woods wandering.

How fortunate was he but lately, and glad,
For Helge and Halfdan as guests he had;
And with the brothers,
Came Ingeborg; Fridthjof scarce saw the others.

He sat by her side and her soft hand he pressed;
He felt in the pressure returned him thrice blest,
Enraptured gazing
On her whom he honored beyond all praising.

In glad conversation recalling their plays,
When life's morning dew presaged bright future days
For memory truthful
Keeps life's rosy gardens in noble minds youthful.

How fondly she greets him from dale and from park,
From loving names growing in White birchen bark,
From hills where flourish
The oaks which the ashes of heroes nourish.

"'Tis never so pleasant at home as here,
For Halfdan is childish and Helge severe;
Tho kings attending
To nothing but prayers and praise unending.

"And no one (nor could she her blushes hide)
To whom my complainings I may confide.
The palace building,
How stifling compared with the groves of Hilding.

"The doves that we petted, and tamed and fed,

By hawks oft affrighted away have fled;
One pair remaineth,
Let Fridthjof take one, one Ing'borg retaineth.

"She'll long like another her friend to see,--
And homeward returning will fly to me:
Your message, bind it
Beneath her flee pinion,--there none will find it."

All day they sat whispering side by side,
Nor ceased the low murmur at eventide;
So breathe in whispers
The zephyrs through lindens at twilight vespers.

But now she has gone, and his joy forsooth
Has gone with the maiden. The blood of youth

His cheek is mounting,
He silently sighs while the past recounting.

His grief at her absence he sent by the dove,
Which joyous set out with its message of love;
But oh! new sorrow,
It stayed with its mate, nor returned on the morrow.

His conduct to Bjorn was displeasing; said he:
"What ails our young eagle, he seems to be
Like some shy sparrow,--
Has his breast or his pinion been pierced by an arrow?

"What wilt thou, Fridthjof? We have for need
The yellow bacon, and the good, brown mead;
And poets singing,
Their jubilant music forever ringing.

"The steeds impatiently stamp in the stalls,--
To the chase! to the chase! the falcon calls;
But Fridthjof retaineth
His gloom. He hunteth in clouds and complaineth.

"Ellide is restless upon the main,--
She frets and she chafes at her cable chain;
Lie still my treasure!
Our Fridthjof is peaceable. Strife is no pleasure.

"Who dies on his pallet,, is dead indeed;
By the lance, as did Odin, we'll die, if need,--
And thus ensure us
A welcome to Hel, and heaven secure us."

Then Fridthjof unloos'd the dragon,--and proud,
With full swelling canvas, the waves she plowed,
And swiftly over
The bay to the palace she bore the lover.

The kings were at Bele's grave met that day,--
To administer justice and counsel weigh;
Fridthjof advances,--
His voice sounds afar like clashing lances.

"Ye kings, lovely Ing'borg, the people's pride,
I choose, from all women, to be my bride;
The king intended
Our lives thus united in one should be blended.

"He reared us together in Hilding's sight,--
As two forest saplings whose tops unite,--
A golden cover
Of lace bindeth Freyja the green tops over.

"My sire was a peasant, no earl nor king,--
Yet his memory will live while the poets sing;
In runic story
The grave-mounds are telling my ancestors' glory.

"I could easily win me a crown and land,
But choose to remain on my native strand:
In battle wielding
My sword for the king, and the peasant shielding.

"On king Bele's grave we are standing now,
He hears every word in the grave below,
With me he pleadeth,--

A dead father's counsel a wise son heedeth."

Then Helge uprose, and replied with scorn,
"Our sister was not for a peasant born,
To kings 'tis given
To strive for our Ingeborg, daughter of heaven.

"You boastfully call yourself chief of swords,--
Win men by violence, women bv words;
Boast not of slaughter,
For arrogance winneth not Odin's daughter.

"My kingdom doth not seek protection from thee,
I shield it myself. My man wouldst thou be,--
A situation
Among my domestics befits thy station."

"Thy servant! no, never!" was Fridthjof's reply,
"My father had never a master--shall I?
From thy silver dwelling
Now fly, Angervadil, the insult repelling."

In sunshine now glitters the blue steel blade,--
Displaying its letters in flaming red.
"My good sword loyal,
Thy lineage at least," said Fridthjof, "is royal.

"And were it not now for the high grave's renown,
Right here would I hew thee, swarthy king, down:
Yet will I teach thee
To come not again where my sword can reach thee."

So saying, be severed at one fell blow

The gold shield of Helge which hung on a bough.
It fell asunder,--
Its clang on the grave-mound was echoed under.

"Well done, Angervadil. lie still and dream
Of high achievements,-- meanwhile the gleam
Of rune-fires paling!
And now we'll go home o'er the blue waters sailing."

V.
King Ring.

King Ring moved his gold-stool back. Then uprose
 Champion and dreamer;--
For where in the North does such goodness repose?
His word o'erflows
 With the wisdom which dwells in god Mimer.

Like the groves of the peaceful gods was his land,--
 War's sable pinion
Cast not a shadow where on every hand
Flowers expand
Through the length of his quiet dominion.

Here Justice alone on the judgment-seat
 With Right presided;
And Peace every year paid its tribute meet,--
While golden wheat
 With plenty the harvest provided.

And swarthy-prowed ships to this favored shore,
 With snowy pinions
The products of numberless nations bore,--
A varied store
 Of riches for fortune's rich minions.

Here freedom and peace did in concord dwell,
 Kindly united;
And all loved their father, the king, full well,
For each might tell
 His mind in the thing,[3] none were slighted.

Supreme in the Northland through thirty years
 His reign extended;
Contented each went to his daily cares;
At evening prayers
 The king's name in blessings ascended.

King Ring moved his gold-stool back. From the board
 All there assembled
Arose to attend on the royal word,--
Renowned where heard:
 But he sighed, and in accents that trembled,

He said: "My lost queen is in Folkvang-hall
 On purple seated;
But here on her grave is a grassy pall,
While breathe o'er all
 The flowers with sweet odor freighted.

"So queenly, so honored, so good and so fair,
 There's not another.
Immortal she dwelleth in Valhal's care,
But the people's prayer,
 The children's desire, is a mother.

"King Bele oft sat as a guest at my side

---

3 See glossary

When winter ended;
The daughter he left I would choose for my bride,--
Her father's pride,
   In whose cheeks rose and lily are blended.

"I know she is young, and in youth sublime.
   Would gather flowers;
My flower is past and my early prime;
My locks has Time
   Besprinkled with snowy showers.

Oh, could she but honor the withered tree
   Which age has blighted;
And could she a friend to the motherless be,
Then should you see
   To the throne Spring by Autumn invited.

"Take gold froth my coffers, take jewels rare,
   Unstinted measure
Let minstrels attending the way prepare
To win the fair,--
   For song heralds wooing and pleasure."

With gold and petitions, a noisy throng,
   The young men speeded;
And minstrels and skalds, in procession long,
With hero-song
   To the sons of King Bele proceeded.

The feast, where with wassail they drink and sing,
   For three days lasted,
But they sought the fourth morning what answer they'd bring

From Helge king,--
 For now their return must be hasted.

In the grove Helge offered both bird and beast,--
 A sacred duty;
Asked counsel of vala, consulted the priest
What answer was best
 For the queen of affection and beauty.

The offerings and vala and priest denied
 The wished-for token;
And Helge, affrighted by signs he'd tried,
With "No," replied,
 For men must obey when the gods have spoken.

But merry king Halfdan laughed gayly, and said,
 "The feast is ended,
King Gray-beard himself should have come instead,
I'd glad have led
 His beast, and his mounting attended."

Indignant the embassy went away,
 Nor longer tarried;
"King Graybeard his honor'll avenge one day,"
Is Ring heard to say,
 When to him the curt message is carried.

He strikes his bright shield hanging high on a bough,--
 His weapon seizes;
And many a dragon is hurrying now,
With blood-red prow,
 And helmet plumes wave in the breezes.

The tidings flew swiftly to Helge king,
 Who answered slowly:
"The strife will be bloody, for mighty is Ring;
My sister bring
 To the temple of Balder, the holy."

There sitteth the loving one, full of woes,
 Though safe abiding:
She weeps, while with silk and with god she sews
A tear overflows,--
 The dew 'mid the lilies is hiding.

VI.
Fridthjof Plays Chess

Bjorn and Fridthjof chess were playing
On a board, whose squares displaying
 Gold and silver deftly fitted,
  Skill and beauty both combined.
Then stepped Hilding in. "Come nigher,"
Fridthjof said, "and sit thee higher
 'Till our game shall be completed,--
  Foster-father kind."

Hilding answered: "From the palace
I am come to you for solace.
 Evil are the times at present,
  You are all the people's hope."
Fridthjof said: "The foe encroaches,
Danger, Bjorn, your king approaches;
 You can save him by a peasant.--
  He is nothing, give him up.

"Fridthjof, anger kings no longer,
Lo, the eagle's young grow stronger;
 Ring may thwart, their weak endeavor,
  Thou wilt surely find it hard."
"Bjorn, I see you storm the tower.

And in vain your threatening power
 'Gainst the castle is; it ever
  Safety seeks behind its guard."

"Ing'borg sits in Balder's dwelling,
Grief her constant tears compelling:
 She should make thee seize thy armor
  She with tearful eyes of blue."
"Vain you strive my queen to capture,
Dear from childhood's days of rapture;
 Best of all, there's nought shall harm her
  Come what may, to her I'm true."

"Fridthjof, art thou still unheeding
All thy foster-father's pleading?
 For thy foolish game art ready
  I should go without a word?"
Fridthjof then arises, laying
Hilding's hand in his, and saying:
 "My resolve is firm and steady,
  And my answer you have heard.

"Go to Bele's sons and warn them,
Peasants love not those who scorn them;
 To their power I bid defiance,
  Their behests will not obey."
"In thy chosen way abide thee,
For thy wrath I can not chide thee;
 Odin must be our reliance,"
  Hilding said, and went his way.

VII.
Fridthjof's Happiness.

King Bele's sons may go requesting
 From dale to dale the peasants' aid,
In Balder's grove my world is resting,
 For them I will not draw my blade.
Then on king's vengeance or earth's sadness,
 I will no longer look or think,
But only will the high gods' gladness,
 From out one cup with Ing'borg drink.

While yet the hazy sunshine sendeth
 Its purple rays on flowers at rest,
Like rosy gossamer which lendeth
 An added charm to Ing'borg's breast,
With sighs along the strand I wander,
 My soul with longing all aflame,
Upon the sand I gaze and ponder
 And with my sword write Ing'borg's name.

How slowly go the lonesome hours!
 Thou Delling's son, why stayest thou?
Hast thou not seen our mountain bowers,
 Our lakes and islands until now?
Dwells there in western halls no maiden

Who waits since morn first kissed the sea,
Upon thy breast her joys to unladen,
 Whose whole of life is love and thee?

At last thy footsteps grow uncertain,
 Thy weary journey thou must close,
Now evening draws the rosy curtain,
 Behind whose folds the gods repose.
The brooks and breezes to each other
 In softest whispers love express;
O! welcome Night, of gods the mother,
 With pearls upon thy wedding dress.

The stars are gliding like a lover
 On tiptoe to a maiden true;
Ellide! fly the deep gulf over,
 Roll on, roll on, ye billows blue.
Yon sacred grove a temple hideth,
 Good Balder's temple, doubly dear,
For there love's goddess safe abideth,
 Unto the gods our course we steer.

Thy shores I tread with joyous measure,
 I kiss thy brown cheek, smiling earth,
And all ye little flowers, with treasure
 Of white and red, that edge my path.
I hail thee, moon, with pale light streaming
 On temple-grove and flowers at rest,
How beautiful thou sittest dreaming
 Like Saga at a wedding feast.

To speak with flowers, O, brook, who taught thee
 The feeling in my heart a guest?

Ye northern nightingales, where caught ye
 The wailing stolen from my breast?
With evening's red the fairies playing,
 In clouds my Ing'borg's form disclose,
But Freyja, jealousy displaying.
 Away the image quickly blows.

Though changing clouds lose her resemblance,
 Like radiant hope herself appears,
As true as childhood's sweet remembrance,
 She comes, my love's reward she bears.
Come, loved one, come, and let me press thee
 Unto the heart that holds thee dear,
My soul's desire, through life, I'll bless thee,
 Come to my arms, and rest thee here.

Frail as the lily's stem so slender,
 Yet like spring roses fresh and fair,
As Freyja's troth-plight, warm and tender,
 Thou as the will of gods art pure.
Kiss me, and let my burning passion
 Kindle thy soul to perfect bliss,
Of earth and heaven I lose the vision,
 Enraptured by thy melting kiss.

Fear not, for here can come no stranger,
 Without stands Bjorn. his sword in hand,
His champions guarding ns from danger,
 If need be, can the world withstand;
And I, if fighting for my treasure,
 Whose form I on my bosom bear,
To Valhal now would go with pleasure,
 Could'st then be my valkyrie there.

And why fear Balder's fierce resentment,
 The pious god to whom we pray?
He looks on us with calm contentment,
 For, loving, we his law obey.
The god whose brow with sunshine beameth,
 With whom all truth abideth sure,
His love unto his Nanna seemeth
 Like mine to thee, so warm, so pure.

There stands his image, not indignant,
 But mild and soft as sunset ray,
Upon this shrine of god benignant,
 My heart a sacrifice I lay.
Together let us kneel before him,
 No better offering can be found
Than two fond hearts which both adore him,
 With love like his together bound.

Scorn not my love, my blossom cherished,
 Which more to heaven than earth belongs,
In heaven itself that love was nourished,
 And for that glorious home it longs.
Oh! that my weary soul releasing,
 The gods would take me up above;
Triumphantly, with joy unceasing,
 I'd go, embraced by my dear love.

When bugle-notes the champions rally,
 From out the silver gates they ride;
But I alone join not the sally,
 I linger gladly by thy side.
When Valhal's maidens pass me, smiling,
 The mead-horn with its rim of gold;

Thee, only thee, my love beguiling,
 My tender, loving arms enfold.

A leafy cottage near the meadow
 I'd build us by the dark-blue sea,
And there we'd rest us 'neath the shadow
 Of many a golden-fruited tree;
And when bright Valhal's sun each morning,
 With his clear torch in splendor rose,--
We'd hasten to the gods returning,
 Yet longing for our home's repose.

Thy golden locks, with sunshine flushing,
 Wreathed with a starry crown should be;
So my pale lily, rosy blushing,
 In Vingolf-hall should dance with me.
Then, by my love from danger guarded,
 I'd with thee to our home repair,--
Where singeth Brage, silver-bearded,
 Our wedding song each evening fair.

How sweet the evening song-bird's vesper!
 It cometh forth from Valhal's shore;
How soft the moon-beams' gentle whisper,
 From where the dead live evermore!
They tell of light and love unbroken,
 In homes devoid of care and pain;
Where joyous words alone are spoken,
 There thou my love shalt ever reign.

Oh, weep not, love, those tears regretful,
 While through my heart the life-blood streams;
But sweetly sleep,--of grief forgetful

May love and Fridthjof fill thy dreams.
Oh! when thine arms thou foldest round me,
 When thy dear eyes but look on me,
How quickly breaks the spell that bound me,
 How turn my thoughts from heaven to thee!

"List to the lark's melodious numbers."
 Nay, 'tis a dove his love-song sings,
The lark on yonder hillock slumbers,
 Beside his mate with folded wings.
How happy they, always together,
 As free their life as wings that bear
Through cheerless storm or sunny weather,
 Above the clouds, that happy pair.

"See, daybreak comes." Nay, but ascended
 From some far beacon is the light;
Our happy talk is not yet ended,
 Nor yet so soon the lovely night.
Bright morning stat sleep till to-morrow,
 And when night cometh, slumber still,
Your waking brings to Fridthjof sorrow,--
 So sleep till doomsday, if you will.

Vain hope! No longer earth reposes,
 The morning breeze new pleasure seeks;
Already bud the eastern roses,
 As fresh as those on Ing'borg's checks.
I hear the winged songsters twitter,
 A thoughtless throng in the opening sky;
All life's astir, the wavelets glitter,
 And lover must with shadows fly.

Ah! there he comes, in glory beaming;
 Forgive, O golden sun, my prayer.
How beautiful, in splendor gleaming!
 I feel--I know a god is near.
Oh! who could, in thy path advancing,
 With equal grace and power tread,
All hearts with light and joy entrancing,
 A life like thine victorious lead!

Here, 'neath thy watchful eye I leave her--
 My peerless beauty of the North!
Let not the rough world's troubles grieve her,
 Thy likeness on the green-clad earth.
Her soul is pure as rays of morning,
 Her eyes as blue as thine own sky,

The same rich tints thy crown adorning
 Among her golden tresses lie.

Farewell, my love, be not forgetful,
 Some longer night again we'll meet;
I, lingering, kiss thy brow, regretful,
 One kiss I give thy lips so sweet.
Sleep now, beloved; in thy slumber,
 May dreams of me thy bosom swell,
At mid-day wake, and with me number
 Each absent hour: farewell, farewell.

VIII.
The Parting.

Ingeborg.

The day breaks clear, and Fridthjof cometh not,
Though yesterday the council was proclaimed
At Bele's grave. The place was rightly chosen,
His daughter's fate should be determined there.
How many supplications hath it cost me,
How many tears by Freyja counted o'er,
To melt the ice of hate around Fridthjof's heart.
And gain a promise from his haughty lips
To give his hand in reconciliation.
Alas! how hard is man! And for his honor,
So calleth he his pride, he counts it not,
Or lightly counts it, if he rudely break,
Of true and faithful hearts one more or less.
But wretched woman, leaning on his breast,
Is like the moss-growth blooming on the cliff,--
With faded tints, it difficultly holds
Itself unnoticed fast unto the rock,
Is only nourished by the dews of night.
But yesterday, indeed, my fate was fixed,
And now the evening sun hath set upon it,
Still Fridthjof cometh not. The pallid stars

Die one by one, and sadly disappear,
And with each one of them a hope is quenched
And goes from out my heart unto its grave.
Ah! wherefore still to hope? Valhal's gods
No longer love me; I've offended them.
And Balder, 'neath whose shelter I reside,
Is wroth with me, because a human love
Is too unholy for the sight of gods,
And earthly joy must never risk itself
Beneath the temple-arch in which the grave,
The haughty powers have fixed their dwelling-place.
And yet what fault is mine? and wherefore frowns
The pious god upon a maiden's love?
Is it not pure as Urd's bright sparkling fount,
And innocent as Gefjon's morning dream?
The shining sun doth never turn away
From loving ones, its pure and watchful eyes.
And daylight's widow, starry night, doth hear
With gladness, in her sorrow, all their vows.
That which is worthy under heaven's vault,
Can that be guilty 'neath the temple's dome?
I love my Fridthjof. Oh! through all the past,
As far as memory runs, I loved him well,--
A holy feeling twin-born with my soul,
I know not whence it came, nor comprehend
The dismal thought that it was ever gone.
As fruit is timely set about the stone
And groweth up, and round about it all
In summer sunshine wraps its cloth of gold,
So, too, indeed, have I maturing grown
About this stone, and my existence is
Of my affection but the outer shell.
Forgive me, Balder! With a faithful heart

Thy hall I sought, and with a faithful one
Will I go hence; I'll take it with me now
Out over Bifrost-bridge, and place myself
With all my love before great Valhal's gods.
And there my love, like them an Asa-child,
Shall see itself reflected in the shields,
And fly with loosened dove-wings through the blue
Unending space unto the Allfather's bosom,
From whence it came. Oh! wherefore is the frown,
In morning's twilight, on thy brow so fair?
There floweth in my veins, as flows in thine,
Old Odin's blood. What wilt thou, kinsman dear?
My ardent love I cannot offer thee,
Nor would I offer it, worth all thy joys;
But I can offer thee my life's delight,--
Can cast it from me as the stately queen
Her mantle flings aside, and still remains
Her queenly self. But my resolve is taken,
And Valhal high shall never be ashamed
To own me kindred. I will meet my fate
As meets the hero his. Ah! here he comes!
How wild he seems, how pale! 'Tis done, 'tis done!
My angry norn she comes beside him now:
Be strong, my soul! At last I welcome thee.
Our fate is fixed; 'tis plain to read it where
Upon thy brow it stands.

   Fridthjof.

     And stand not there
As well the blood-red runes, which speak of shame,
And scorn and banishment?

Ingeborg.

Oh, Fridthjof; think! Relate what passed, for I have long foreseen
The worst, and am prepared for all.

Fridthjof.

I found the council at our fathers' graves.
Around the grassy mounds, shield meeting shield,
Stood many Northland sons with swords in hand,
One circle standing close within another
Unto the top. Upon the judgment seat,
A thunder cloud, thy brother Helge sat,--
A pallid headsman with a dusky look.
And next to him, a seeming grown up child,
Sat Halfdan,---thoughtless, playing with his sword.
Then I arose, and, said: "War waiting stands
Within thy borders, beating on the shield,--
Thy kingdom now, king Helge, is in peril;
Give me my sister, and I'll give to thee
Mine arm, it may be useful] in this strife.
Between us let ill will forgotten be,--
I would not cherish it 'gainst Ing'borg's brother.
To reason listen, king, and save at once
Thy golden crown, thy purest sister's heart.
Here is my hand. By Asa-Thor, I swear,
I'll never offer it again to thee."
An uproar shook the thing. A thousand swords
Approval hammered on a thousand shields.
The clang of weapons flew to heaven, which heard
With joy the assent of freemen to the right.
"To him give Ingeborg, the slender lily,
Most beautiful our dales have ever grown;

No better sword our favored land can boast,--
To him give Ingeborg." Our foster-father,
The reverend Hilding, with his silver-beard,
Stood forth and spoke in words of wisdom full,
Short apothegms, as keen as sharpened swords.
And Halfdan, too, from off of royal seat
Arose, with pleading words and pleading looks,--
But it was all in vain; each prayer was wasted,--
Like sunshine lavished on a barren rock,
No growth alluring from his stony heart.
King Helge's sullen countenance was like
His heart,--a pale-faced "No" to human prayers.
"A peasant's son," said he, contemptuously,
"Could Ing'borg gain, but who profanes the temple
Ill-suited seems to holy Valhal's daughter.
Hast thou not, Fridthjof, broken Balder's peace?
Hast thou not seen my sister in his temple
When day had hid itself from your communion?
Say yes, or no!" A deafening shout resounded
From all those rings of men: "Say no, say no,
We take thee at thy word, we sue for thee,--
Thou son of Thorstein, equal to a king;
Say no, say no, and Ingeborg is thine!"
"My life's delight hangs on a feeble word,"
Said I, "but fear it not, king Helge!
I would not lie myself to Valhal's joy,
Much less to earth's. Thy sister I have seen,
Have talked with her beneath the temple's night,
But Balder's peace I have not therefore broken."
They let me say no more. Abhorrent cries
Flew through the thing, and those who nearest stood
Drew back as from a pestilent disease;
And when I looked around, their superstition

Had palsied every tongue, and blanched each cheek
So lately glowing with expectant joy.
And then king Helge triumphed. With a voice
As sad, as awful as the ghostly vala's
In Vegtam's song, when she for Odin sung
Of asas' fate and grim Hel's victory,
So sad he spoke: "Though banishment or death
I could decree, by our ancestral laws
Against this crime, yet I'll be mild as Balder,
Whose sacred dwelling thou hast so profaned.
The western sea a wreath of islands holds,
Where Angantyr, the earl, is governor.
As long as Bele lived the earl each year
His tribute paid, but ceased when Bele died.
Go o'er the sea and drive this tribute in;
This penance thy audacity demands.
'Tis said," sneered he, with meanest mockery,
"That Angantyr hard-fisted is, and broods
Like dragon Fafner o'er his gold: but who
Can stand 'gainst our new Sigurd, Fafner's bane?
Exploits more manly must thou undertake
Than luring maidens under Balder's roof.
When summer comes shall we expect you here
With all thy honor, first of all the tribute.
If not, thou art to every man a felon,
And during life art outlawed through the land."
His judgment rendered, he dissolved the thing.

Ingeborg.

And your decision?

Fridthjof.

       Have I aught to choose?
Is not mine honor bound by his decree?
And that will I redeem though Angantyr
His paltry gold doth hide in Nastrand's flood.
To-day will I depart.

  Ingeborg.

        And Ing'borg leave?

  Fridthjof.

Nay, nay, I leave thee not, thou goest too.

  Ingeborg.

Impossible!

  Fridthjof.

      O! hear me, ere thou answerest.
Thy crafty brother seemeth to forget,
That Angantyr was my dear father's friend,
As well as Bele's. Perhaps he'll give
Without constraint what I demand; if not
A worthy advocate, a sharp one too,
Have I. 'Tis always ready at my side.
The gold he covets I'll to Helge send,
And thus will I from sacrificial knife
Of this crowned hypocrite redeem us both.
But we, my beauteous Ingeborg, will spread

O'er seas unknown Ellide's willing sail,
She'll kindly bear us to a friendlier strand
Where exiled love may safe asylum find.
What is the North to me? And what a race,
Which pales at every word of priest or king,
Whose shameless hands would pluck the living rose
From out the sanctuary of my heart?
So, Freyja help, it shall not prosper them!
The wretched slave is bound unto the turf
Where he was born, hut I will still be free,
Free as the mountain winds. A little earth
From Bele's grave and from my father's taken,
Can find a place ,upon our ship, and that
Is all of fatherland that we can need.
My loved one, there another sun is found
Than that which pales above these hills of snow,
And there another sky, more bright than this;
And milder stars with god-like glance adorned,
Look down therefrom in balmy summer nights
On lovers wandering in the laurel groves.
My father, Thorstein, Viking's son, in wars
Had journeyed far, and oft I've heard him tell,
By fireside light in winter evenings long,
About the Grecian sea with islands filled,--
Fresh groves of green in brightly shining waves.
A powerful race once had its dwelling there,--
And holy gods the marble temples graced.
But now they stand deserted; grasses thrive
In paths left desolate, and flowers grow
From out the runes that tell of ancient lore;
The slender columns stand like budding trees
Entwined by graceful stems of southern vines.
Throughout the year the earth spontaneous yields,

In unsown harvests, all that men require.
There golden apples glow between the leaves,
And blushing grapes from every bough hang down
And, ripening, swell luxurious as thy lips.
There, Ing'borg, there we'll build us near the wave
A little North, more beautiful than this;
And with our ever faithful love we'll fill
The radiant temple vaults, and thus delight
With human fondness the forgotten gods.
And when, with loosened sheets (no storms are there)
The sailor idly floats along our isle
In twilight's glow, and turns his joyous glance
From rosy-colored ripples to the strand,--
Upon the temple's threshold shall he see
A second Freyja, Aphrodite called
In southern tongue, and he shall wonder at
The golden locks, seen flowing in the breeze,
And eyes which brighter gleam than southern skies.
And one by one around her groweth up
A little temple-dwelling race of fairies,
With cheeks where yon might see the south had set,
In Northern snowdrifts, freshly blooming roses.
Ah! Ingeborg, how beautiful, how near.
Stands earthly happiness to faithful hearts;
If they are brave enough to seize it when disposed,

It follows willingly and builds for them
A Vingolf even here beneath the clouds.
O come, let's haste away, each spoken word
A moment shorter makes our waiting joy.
Come, all's prepared! Ellide stretches now
Her shadowy eagle wings for eager flight,--
And freshly blowing winds now guide the way

Henceforth from this inconstant land forever.
Why tarriest thou?

   Ingeborg.

       I cannot follow thee.

   Fridthjof.

Not follow me?

   Ingeborg.

       Ah! Fridthjof, thou art blest!
Thou followest none, but always in the front,
The stem of thy good dragon ship, dost place
Thy will beside the helm, to steer the way
With steady hand above the wrathful waves.
How widely different the case with me!
My cruel fate is held in other's hands,
Which loosen not the prey although it bleed;
And sacrifice, lament and lonesome pining,
Is all king Bele's daughter knows of freedom.

   Fridthjof.

Art thou not free, if so thou willest? In the grave
Thy father sits.

   INGEBORG,

       No, Helge is my father,
Is in my father's stead; on his consent

My hand depends, and Ing'borg will not steal
Her happiness, however near it stands.
Ah! what would woman be if she cut loose
The sacred band with which the Allfather binds
Unto the stronger power her gentle being?
The water-lily pale resembles her;
It rises with the wave and with it falls.
The sailor's keel goes forward over it
And marks it not although it cut the stem.
Such is indeed her fate! And yet the flower,
As long as clings the root unto the sand,
Its growth increases, borrowing color pure
From its pale sister stars which shine above,--
Itself a star upon the waters blue.
But rudely broken loose, it ceaseless drives,
A withered leaf along deserted waves.
Last night,--that was indeed a fearful night,
An unrewarded watch I kept for thee,
And children of the night, the serious thoughts,
With raven locks went thronging closely by
My ever watchful, burning, tearful eyes;
And Balder too, the bloodless god looked down
On me with frowning glances full of threats.
Last night I pondered o'er my wretched fate.
My resolution's taken; I remain
Obedient victim at my brother's altar.
Yet it is well I did not hear thee then,
With fabled islands floating in the clouds
Where evening's glowing twilights always show
A flowery world of peace and happy love.
Who knows how weak one is? My childhood dreams
Though silent long, with joy rise up again,
And whisper in my anxious ear with voice

Familiar as a sister's kindly tones,
As tender as a lover's ardent praise.
I hear ye not! ah, no, I hear ye not,
Alluring accents once so fondly loved!
A child of Northland cannot elsewhere dwell;
Too pale am I for those bright summer roses;-
Too colorless my mind for that deep glow;
The scorching sun would quite consume me there.
Of anxious longing full, my eyes would seek
The northern star which always watchful stands
A heavenly sentry o'er our fathers' graves.
My noble Fridthjof shall not now desert
The cherished hind that he was born to guard;
He shall not fling away his honored name
To gain so poor a thing, a maiden's love.
A life where spins the sun from year to year,
And where each day is ever like the next--
A beauteous but unending sameness, is
For woman only, but for manly souls,
And most for thine, it's quiet, weary dullness.
Thou thrivest best where storms are raging round.
On foaming pacers o'er the heaving sea,
And on thy tossing plank, come life or death,
Thou mayest fight with peril for thine honor.
The beauteous desert thou dost paint, would be
A grave for high achievements, not yet born;
And like thy shield, with rust would be dissolved,
Thine independent mind. It shall not be!
I will not steal away my Fridthjof's name
From poet's storied song; I will not quench
My hero's glory in its morning dawn.
Be wise, my Fridthjof; let us yield unto
The haughty norn; let us rescue yet

Our cherished honor from this wreck of life;
Our happiness we cannot save, 'tis gone,
And separate we must!

   Fridthjof.

           And wherefore must?
Because a sleepless night disturbed thy mind?

   Ingeborg.

Because my honor must be saved, and thine.

   Fridthjof.

A woman's honor rests on manly love.

   Ingeborg.

Not long loves he whom he cannot respect.

   Fridthjof.

Respect is not by fickle fancy gained.

   Ingeborg.

A sense of justice is a noble fancy.

   Fridthjof.

Our love strove not with justice yesterday.

Ingeborg.

Nor love to day, but all the more our flight.

Fridthjof.

Necessity commands our flight,--Oh, come!

Ingeborg.

What's right and noble, that's necessity.

Fridthjof.

High rides the sun and time is fleeting by.

Ingeborg.

Ah, me, it has gone by, gone by forever!

Fridthjof.

Consider well. Is that thy last resolve?

Ingeborg.

I have considered well; it is my last.

Frydthjof.

Farewell then, fare thee well, king Helge's sister.

Ingeborg.

Oh, Fridthjof! Fridthjof! must we separate thus?
Hast thou indeed no friendly glance to give
Thy childhood's friend; no kindly hand to reach
To the unfortunate, once so beloved?
Think'st thou I stand on roses here, and turn
Away with smiles my happiness for life?
And that I pangless tear from out my breast
A hope that hath with my affections grown?

Oh! wert thou not my heart's own morning dream?
Each joy that I have known was Fridthjof named,
And all of life that great or noble seemed,
Did Fridthjof's likeness take before mine eyes.
Bedim the image not: oh, do not meet
With cruelty the weak one offering up
The dearest thing upon the face of earth.
The dearest thing that Valhal's gods can give!
That offering, Fridthjof, is severe enough.
And words of consolation well deserves.
I know thou lovest me--that I have known
E'er since my being first began to dawn;
And Ing'borg's thoughts will surely follow thee
For years to come wherever thou may'st go.
The clang of warlike weapons deadens grief.
'Tis blown away upon the wild, wild waves,
Nor ventures to return when champions all
Their victory celebrate with drinking horn.
Yet sometimes, then, when in the peace of night,
Thy thoughts review again forgotten days,
There will among them glide an image pale,
Thou knowest well; it fondly greeteth thee

From regions dear; it is the image of
That virgin pale in Balder's holy grove.
Thou must not drive it thence away, although
It looketh sorrowful, but whisper kind
Into its ear a friendly word; the winds
Of night on faithful wings will bear it me;
One comfort yet, I have none else beside.
For me there's naught to dissipate my grief;
In all surrounding me it hath a tongue;
The holy temple vaults speak but of thee:
The temple's God, which should all threatening seem,
Thy likeness takes when shines the streaming moon.
Behold the sea--there swam thy keel through foam
To her who on the strand awaited thee;
Behold the woods--there stand so many stems
With Ing'borg's runes engraven in the bark;
Now grows the bark and wears away my name,
And that betokens death, the sagas say.
I ask the day when last it saw thy form,
I ask the night, but both are silent still:
And e'en the sea which bears thee, gives reply
But with a solemn sigh along the shore.
With evening's ruddy glow I'll send to thee
A greeting, when it sinks into thy waves.
And heaven's long ship, the fleeting cloud, shall take
On board the wail of the abandoned one.
So shall I sit within my virgin bower,
In mourning clad, of all life's joy bereft,
And broken lilies sew into the cloth,
Until the Spring its cloth doth weave, and sew
It full of better lilies on my grave.
And when I sadly take the harp to sing
Unending sorrow in profoundest tones,

Then burst the burning tears as now--

    Fridthjof.

Thou conquerest, Bele's daughter, weep no more!
Forgive my wrath, it was alone my sorrow
Which for a moment took a wrathful dress, -
A wrathful dress it cannot long endure.
Thou art my kindest norn, my Ingeborg.
A noble mind best teaches what is noble.
Necessity's real wisdom cannot have
A fairer, better advocate than thou,
Thou beauteous vala with the rosy lips!
I yield indeed unto necessity;
I part with thee but part not with my hope;
I'll take it with me over western waves,
I'll take it with me to the gates of death.
The nearest spring-day sees me here again:
King Helge, so I hope, shall see me too.
Then from my promise freed, his bidding done,
The calumny against me, too, atoned,
Then I'll request thee,--nay but I'll demand
In open council and with naked swords,
And not of Helge but of Northland's sons.
Who only can dispose a princess' hand;
I have a word for him who dare refuse.
Farewell till then; be true, forget me not,
And take in memory of our childhood's love,
My arm-ring here, a beauteous Volund-work,
With heaven's wonders graven in the gold;
The best of wonders is a faithful heart.
How well it suits thine arm so snowy-white--
A glow-worm coiled around the lily's stem!

Farewell, my bride, my loved one, fare thee well.
Ere many moons our mournful lot will change.

[He goes.]

Ingeborg.

How glad, how trusting, and of hope how full!
He sets the glittering point of his good sword
Against the norns, and says: "Ye must retreat!"
Thou wretched Fridthjof, the norns will ne'er retreat;
They go their way and laugh at Angervadil.
How little knowest thou my gloomy brother.
Thy brave, heroic temper fathoms not
The awful depths of his, nor understands
The hate that in his envious bosom burns.
His sister's hand he'll never give to thee;
He'd sooner give his crown, pour out his life,
Of me an offering make to Odin old,
Or to old Ring, whom now he fights against.
Wherever I may look, no hope is found,--
Yet am I glad hope lives within thy breast.
In secret will I keep my poor heart's wound,
And pray that all the good gods follow thee.
Here on thine arm-ring can I reckon up
Each separate month of all this lonesome sorrow.
In two, four, six,--then can'st thou come again,
But can'st not find again thine Ingeborg.

IX.
INGEBORG'S LAMENT.

Autumn has come;
Storming now heaveth the deep sea with foam,
Yet would I gratefully lie there,
Willingly die there.

Long gleamed his sail,
Flying to westward before the fierce gale;
Fortunate, Fridthjof to follow
O'er the wild billow.

Swell not so high,
Billows of blue with your deafening cry!
Stars lend assistance, a shining
Pathway defining.

With the spring doves
Fridthjof will come, but the maiden he loves
Cannot in hall or dell meet him,
Lovingly greet him.

Buried she sleeps,
Dead for her love's sake, or bleeding she weeps,
Heart-broken, given by her brother
Unto another.

Falcon he left,
Mine shalt thou be, winged hunter bereft;
I for thy owner will heed thee,
Lovingly feed thee.

Here on his hand~
'Broidering I'll picture thee on the cloth's rand,
Silvery pinions I'll give thee,
Golden claws weave thee.

Once, it is said,
Freyja with falcon-wings north and south sped,
Seeking for Oder, her lover,
All the world over.

Vainly I seek
Wings of the falcon, for mortals too weak.
Only in passing death's portal
Soareth a mortal.

Sit here with me,
Beautiful hunter and look at the sea;--
Longing and looking forever
Bringeth him never.

Dead shall I be,
When Fridthjof comes again over the sea;
Bear thou my love for his weeping,
I shall be sleeping.

X.
FRIDTHJOF AT SEA.

On shore king Helge stood,
By turns he sang and prayed,
And in embittered mood
Besought the goblins' aid.

See! the heavens with darkness toiling,
 Empty space with thunders boom,
Lo, the furious waves are boiling,
 Ocean's surface hid with foam.
Lightnings now the clouds are streaking,
 Here and there a bloody rand,
All the sea-fowls now are shrieking.
 Hasting to the safer strand.

"Hard's the weather, brothers!
Hear the stormy pinions
Flapping in the distance,
Yet we do not pale.
Sit within the temple,
Think on me with longing,
Beauteous in thy weeping,
Beauteous Ingeborg."

'Gainst Ellide's stem,
  Two goblins warfare made.
 One was wind-cold Ham,
  One was snowy Heyd.

Now the storm-wind wildly drifts them
 O'er the deep, and madly down;
Now it beating, whirling lifts them,
 Upward where the heavens frown.
All the powers of evil coming,
 Riding on the billows' top,
From the bottomless, the foaming,
 From the wide graves up.

"Brighter was the journey
 By the pale moon's glimmer,
 Over mirrored waters
 Unto Balder's grove;
 Warmer was it, nearer
 Ing'borg's heart reposing;
 Whiter than the sea-foam
 Swelled her bosom fair."

 Solund island fair
 Above the waves so white!
 Stiller seas are there,
 Harbors safe invite.

But the bold sea-rover feareth
 Less upon the trusted oak,
Mans the helm himself and jeereth
 At the wild wind's sportive stroke.

Tighter now the sail he fastens,
 Fleeter o'er the water skims,
Straight to westward fearless hastens,
 Goes where'er the billow swims.

"Fighting for a moment
 With the storm delighteth:
Storm and Northman prosper
 Well upon the wave.

Ingeborg would redden
 Should her sea-eagle fly with
Slackened wings, affrighted
 By a passing breeze."

Higher rise the waves,
 Deeper furrows plow,
 Cordage madly raves,
 Creak both keel and prow.

Waves whichever way contending,
 With or 'gainst Ellide's form,
Meet good timbered sides, defending
 Menaced ship, defying storm.
Like an evening meteor sweeping,
 Joyful glides she through the night,
Like an Alpine roebuck leaping
 Over precipice and height.

"Better was it kissing
 her in Balder's temple,
Than to stand here tasting

Salt-foam as it whirls.

Better 'twas embracing
Bele's royal daughter
Than to stand here gripping
Fast the rudder's helm."

From the cold sky's field
Snows intense prevail,
And on deck and shield
Rattling storms of hail.

Lo, o'er all the vessel flying
 Night has placed her sable pall,
As in rooms where dead are lying,
 Gloomy darkness covers all.
Wave implacable now lashes
 Toward his doom the sailor brave
White-gray as with sifted ashes
 Frightful yawns a boundless grave.

"Pillows Ran is making,
 Luring us to quiet;
Thine I know are waiting,
 Ingeborg, for me.

Faithful men are plying
Oars of good Ellide;
Gods the keel have made us,
Bear us yet awhile."

See the sea advances,
Seeking now a wreck,
Ere the eye can glance,
Clears the starboard deck.

Fridthjof's sinewy arm adorning,
 Shone a massive golden ring,
Bright its rays of early morning,
 'Twas the gift of Bele, king.
This in many pieces broken,--
 Made by dwarfs with skillful art,--
Gives to all on board a token.
 Every man receives a part.

"Gold is good to carry
When you go a-wooing,
Empty-handed no one
Comes to sea-blue Ran.

Cold is she to kisses,
Flee'th from embraces,
But the sea-bride yieldeth
Met with shining gold."

Now with threatenings new
 Falls the frozen storm,
Rends his sail in two,
 Snaps the brittle arm.

O'er Ellide's side prevailing
 Entering rolls the mountain wave,
Men of giant strength are bailing,

'Gainst, the sea make battle brave.
Fridthjof cannot fail discerning
 That he carries death on board;
Then above the billows storming
 Rises his commanding word.

"Bjorn, attend the rudder,
 Grip it with a bear's paw;
Valhal's holy powers
 Never sent such storm.

Goblins rule the voyage;
 Coward Helge chanted
Safety o'er the waters;
 I will up and see."

Like a bird he flew
 Up the icy spar,
Sat on high to view
 Fiendish goblins war.

See, before Ellide gliding,

 Like an island floating free,
Sea-whale on whose back are riding,
 Loathsome goblins of the sea.
Heyd a snowy pelt, doth cover,
 Figure like a polar bear;
Ham hath wings which, waving hover
 Eagle-like in stormy air.

"Now. Ellide, ready!
 Show if hero temper

Dwells within your banded
Convex breast of oak.

Listen to my order;
Are you Valhal's daughter?
Strike with keel of copper,
Gore the conjured whale!"

Brave Ellide hears
Fridthjof's proud behest.
With a spring she rears
'Gainst the monster's breast.

From the wound a stream is driving,
 To the skies 'tis quickly sped,
Now the wounded monster diving,
 Roaring seeks his miry bed.
Fridthjof's giant strength then casteth
 Lances at the goblins bold,
One in Ice-bear's bosom fasteneth,
 One Storm-eagle's breast doth hold.

"Bravely done, Ellide!
Not so quickly riseth
Helge's magic dragon
Up from out the mire.

Ham and Heyd no longer
Rule the sea together;
Bitter is it biting
'Gainst the dark-blue steel."

Quickly disappears
Storm from sea and land,
Gentle wavelet steers
Toward the nearing strand.

All at once the sun advances,
Like a king doth he unveil,
All enlivens, all entrances,
Ship and billow, mount and dale.
Last rays, gleaming now like amber,
Tops of cliff and forest bound,
Now each sailor well remembers
The emerald shores of Efje Sound.

"Ingeborg, pale maiden,
Prayers sent unto Valhal;
Lily-white she bowed her
Knees on sacred gold.

Light-blue eyes in weeping,
Breast of swan's down, sighing,
Moved the hearts of asas;
Let us give them thanks."

Now Ellide leaks,
Faithful dragon ship,
Shallow water seeks.--
Wearied of the trip.

Still more tired by labor dreary,
Fridthjof's men desire the land;

But enfeebled, faint and weary,
 Sword-supported, scarce can stand.
Bjorn, on powerful shoulders, beareth
 Four of them and safely lands;
Fridthjof, too, the labor shareth,
 Eight sets round the burning brands.

"Do not bhtsh, pale heroes!
Waves are sturdy vikings;
Hard indeed is fighting
'Gainst the ocean's bride.

See, there comes the mead-horn,
Gold the feet that bear it.
Warm your frozen members;
Skoal to Ingeborg!

XI.
FRIDTHJOF WITH ANGANTYR.

'Tis now to tell the story
 How in his fir-wood hall,
Sat Angantyr, the hoary,
 And drank with champions all.
He, joyous and light-hearted,
 Looked out to where the sun
Behind the waves departed,
 Just like a golden swan.

Outside the hall's commotion
 Old Halvard watched,--indeed
Not only watched the ocean,
 But also watched his mead.
His custom, seldom broken,
 Was, quick the horn to drain,
And ere a word was spoken,
 To thrust it in again.

But now he threw it; striding

 Into the hall he spake:
"I see the billows riding
 A ship, whose timbers shake;

I see some sailors dying
  Already on the strand,
And two strong giants, trying
  To bring the rest to land."

O'er waves no longer foaming,
  The noble earl looked out:
"That is Ellide coming,
  And Fridthjof too, no doubt;
His step, so firm and steady,
  Bespeaks him Thorstein's son.
Such brow, and smile so ready,
  In Northland there is none."

Then viking Atle sturdy
  Sprang up at one swift bound;
Black-bearded berserk, bloody,
  And fiercely looked around.
"Now, I will prove," he thunders,
  "What rumor means by this,
That all blades Fridthjof sunders,
  And never sues for peace."

And with the doughty viking,
  His twelve best champions start,
And in the air sharp striking,
  They brandish sword and dart.
They storm the strand, where by it
  The weary dragon lay;
But Fridthjof, sitting nigh it,
  Looks ready for the fray.

"Quite easy could I fell thee,"

The noisy Atle cries:
"No one comes here, I tell thee,
 But either fights or flies.
If peace thou ask'st, believe me,--
 I fight, but am no churl,--
In friendship I'll receive thee,
 And lead thee to the earl."

"Although I'm scarcely rested,"
 Is Fridthjof's sharp reply,
"Our good swords must be tested,
 Before for peace I cry."
Then swift the sun-brown fighter
 His flashing sword-blade swung,
Bright glowed the runes and brighter
 On Angervadil's tongue.

Blows fell without cessation,
 Now deadly blows like rain,
And now in quick rotation
 Each shield is cleft in twain.
Unhurt, with wrath unspoken
 They stand within the ring,--
Now Atle's sword is broken
And Fridthjof's sword is king.

Said he: "A swordless foeman
 I've no desire to slay;
But if you will, as yeomen,
 We'll try another way."
As waves 'gainst waves are pushing,
 And breaking crest on crest,
So on each other rushing,

They wrestled breast to breast.

They fought like two bears trying
 Their strength on crust of snow,
Or, as o'er mad waves flying
 The eagle meets his foe.
The firm earth trembled round them,
 Though based on solid rock,
And oaks, though strong roots bound them,
 Could scarce withstand the shock.

Their brows with sweat were beaded,
 Their breasts heaved with a sound,
The brush and stones unheeded,
 They scattered all around.
The twelve in expectation
 Stood quaking on the sand;
Renowned through every nation
 That struggle on the strand.

But Fridthjof was the stronger,
 He felled his foe at last,
And said with fiery anger,
 His knee on Atle's breast:
"Had I my good sword ready,
 Thou berserk blackbeard, now
Thy miserable body
 I'd straightway plunge it through."

"Go bring it! Who'll prevent thee?"
 Is generous Atle's cry,
"And if it will content thee,
 As now I'll quiet lie.

Why should it make me sorrow?
 For all must Valhal see;
I go to-day--to-morrow
 Perhaps thy turn will be."

Then Fridthjof quick returning,
 Desired to end the fray;
Raised Angervadil burning,--
 But Atle quiet lay.
The falling blade ne'er harmed him,
 For Fridthjof struck the sand;
Such courage had disarmed him,
 He took brave Atle's hand.

With gleeful admonition
 Old Halvard swung his staff:
"For your battle-meal potation
 There's nothing here to quaff;
Upon the board hot-smoking
 The silver dishes glow;
A cold meal is provoking,
 And thirst annoys me so.'

Appeased, with friendly feeling,
 The portals they pass through,
And here from floor to ceiling,
 To Fridthjof all was new.
Rough planks well matched together
 Lined not the spacious hall,
But 'broidered golden leather
 Was stretched along the wall.

The center was not littered

By mortared hearthstone wide;
A marble fireplace glittered,
 Built up against the side.
No smoke 'mid rafters flitted,
 No roof with soot spread o'er;
Glass panes the windows fitted,
 A lock secured the door.

No woollen torches crackling,
 Illumed the champions' feast,
But waxen candles, sparkling,
 In silver sconces placed.
A roasted stag, well larded,
 The table's center graced;
Gold bands his raised hoof guarded,
 With flowers his horns were dressed.

Beside each champion sitting,
 A youthful maiden stood,--
An evening star, bright flitting,
 Behind a stormy cloud
The blue eyes beamed, in showers
 The gold-brown tresses flowed,
Complete as sculptured flowers
 The little rose-lips glowed.

On silver stool, high mounted,
 Sat Angantyr, the old;
His helm shot rays uncounted,
 His corselet was of gold.
His mantle, rich and splendid,
 With golden stars was strewn,--
And where the purple ended,

The spotless ermine shone,

Three steps the earl descended
 To Fridthjof genially
He said, with hand extended:
 "Come higher, sit by me.
Of horns I've emptied many
 With Thorstein in his day;
His son, more famed than any,
 Shall not sit far away."

He filled each goblet brimming

 With wine from Sicily,--
Like sparks of fire 'twas gleaming,
 And foaming like the sea.
"Welcome!" exclaimed the speaker,
 "My friend's most worthy son!
To Thorstein fill a beaker,--
 And drink now, every one!"

Now woke the harpstring's slumbers,
 A skald from Morven's hills,
In Gaul's melodious numbers,
 Sad hero-songs he trills.
But Thorstein's praise was chanted
 In old Norwayan tongue;
His noble deeds were vaunted,
 His daring valor snug.

The earl asked much concerning
 His friends of days gone by;
In words replete with learning

Young Fridthjof made reply.
A judgment given blindly,
Swift accusation brings,
He spoke like Saga, kindly,
Remembering holy things.

And when he there recounted
 How Helge goblins sent,
Which first the blue waves mounted,
 Then, conquered, downward, went,
The champions cheered him loudly,
 And Angantyr the same,--
In high approwd, proudly,
 They echoed Fridthjof's name.

But when he spoke in anguish,
 Of Ing'borg in her bloom,
How she was left to languish,
 Her heart with grief o'ercome,--
Each maiden's cheek was burning,
 Each bosom sore distressed;
And to her lover turning,
 His faithful hand she pressed.

His embassy to mention
 He ventured by and by;
The earl gave pleased attention,
 And then he made reply:
"I ne'er was tributary;
 King Bele's health, maybe,
To drink was customary,
 But from his law we're free.

"His sons, I do not know them;
 If tribute they demand,
Custom the way will show them,
 We'll meet them on the strand,
And see who best is reckoned;
 But Thorstein was my friend."
His daughter then he beckoned,
 Who sat quite near at hand.

Then rose the maiden tender,
 From stool all golden bound,
Her waist is trim and slender,
 Her bosom full and round,
Each dimpled cheek encloses
 An Astrild, roguish sprite,
As when on opening roses,
 The butterflies alight.

She hastened to her bower,
 A green silk purse she brought,
With bird and tree and flower
 And beast 'twas deftly wrought;
On seas were white-winged vessels,
 Beneath the silver moon,
Of gold were all the tassels,
 The clasp with rubies shone.

She placed the dainty treasure
 Within her father's band;
He filled it, brimming measure,
 With coin from foreign land.
"This welcome gift is only
 A tribute to a friend;

And now the winter lonely
  Consent with us to spend.

True courage knows no danger,
  But Heyd and Ham, I fear,
Revived await the ranger,
  And winter storms are here.
All foes the deep is hiding,
  Ellide may not shun,
And many whales are riding
  The waves, though conquered one."

With jesting and potation
  The hours till day were spent,
Without inebriation
  The wine-cup gladness lent.
A brimming skoal was given
  To Angantyr at last;
So Fridthjof in this haven
  The cheerful winter passed.

XII.
THE RETURN.

Now spring is breathing in skies of blue,
And earth her carpet has woven anew,
And Fridthjof grateful his kind host leaving
Again the billowy plain is cleaving,
And gayly speeding through silver-spray,
His black swan ploweth her sunny way.

The western breezes that spring is bringing,
Like nightingales in the sails are singing,
And AEger's daughters in veils of blue
About the rudder their sports pursue.
Ah, how delightful when safely clearing
A foreign land, to be homeward steering!
When memory pictures the smoke that curled
Above one's hearthstone, his childhood's world,
The fount where playing his swift feet hurried,
The honored graves where his dead are buried.
He thinks of her who perchance may be
On high cliffs standing to watch the sea.
Six days he sailed on his way returning,
The seventh a strip of blue discerning
Low down the horizon, he neared it fast,
Saw rock and islet and land at last.
That land is his; from the waves advancing,

He sees green forests in sunlight dancing.
He hears the roar of the foaming streams,
Can trace each cliff which with granite gleams,
Salutes the headland and sound, then glideth
Along by the groves where his Ing'borg bideth.
Thinks how last summer each evening fair,
With her beside him he wandered there.
"Where is she? Guesses she not her lover
Is near her, safely the blue waves over?
Perhaps, removed from her Balder's care,
She strikes the harp in the palace, where
Her grief she'd lessen, her needle plying."

Then sudden rises his falcon, flying
From temple turret, then downward flits
To Fridthjof's shoulder, and there he sits,
As was his wont, of his love to assure him.
From Fridthjof's shoulder can none allure him,
He scratches fast with his gold-tipped claws,
He gives no quiet, he makes no pause.
To Fridthjof's ear now his beak he bendeth,
Perchance some loved one a message sendeth;
Is it Ingeborg? Wildly his pulses bound,
But none interprets the broken sound.

Ellide gayly the headland rounding,
Skips lightly on, like a roebuck bounding.
Familiar waters surround the prow
Where happy Fridthjof is standing now.
He rubs his eyes and his hand he places
Above his brow to discern the traces
Of home so dear; but he looks in vain,--
Of Framness ashes alone remain.

The naked chimney stands lone and dreary,
Like warriors' bones of their grave-mounds weary;
The garden place is a blackened floor,
The ashes whirl round the wasted shore.
In bitter mood from his ship he hasteth,
Around the ruins his eyes he casteth,
His father's dwelling, his childhood's pride.
Then faithful Bran with the shaggy hide,
Comes running toward him, each moment faster,--
Of forest bears had he oft been master;
How high he springs in his gladsome glee,
How leaps with pleasure his friend to see.
The milk-white steed he so oft had ridden
Comes bounding up from the valley hidden,
With swan-like neck and the frame of a hind
And gold mane floating upon the wind.
He curves his neck and he stamps while standing,
His food from Fridthjof's own hand demanding;
But Fridthjof, poorer by far than they,
Has nought to give them,--he turns away.

Unsheltered, sorrowful stands the rover;
He looks at the meadow and grove burnt over,-
Of Hilding's coming quite unaware,
His foster-father with silver hair.
"At what I see I can scarcely wonder,
When eagles flit then their nests are plunder.
'Tis Helge's deed lest the land be wroth,
So well he keeps his crowning oath!
To hate mankind and to gods be loyal,
While blackened homes mark his progress royal!
More grief it gives me and less of pain;
But where does my Ingeborg meanwhile remain?"

"The word I hear," Hilding said in sadness,
"I fear will bring you but little gladness.
You scarce had sailed when king Ring came on,
Five shields I counted against our one.
In Disar-dale did we prove our valor,--
The river foamed with a crimson color.
King Halfdan's jest and his laugh arose,
So too the sound of his manly blows.
My shield I held as a buckler o'er him,
Well pleased with fruits his bravery bore him.
Not long indeed did the battle last.
King Helge yielded, and flying fast,
Though asa-blood in his veins was welling,
In passing Framness he fired the dwelling.
Before the brothers the choice was placed,
To give their sister to Ring, disgraced.
(By her alone could his wrongs be righted),
Or give their throne for his offer slighted.
Then hither and thither the messengers hied,
But now has Ring carried home his bride."

"O woman, woman!" said Fridthjof, scorning,
"Old Loke's thought should have been a warning;
His thought a lie, was in woman's form,
To man he sent it his heart to warm,
A blue-eyed lie that with tears alarms us,
Forever cheats and forever charms us;
A rose-checked lie with bust defined,
Of spring-ice virtue and faith like wind;
From out whose heart folly often glances,
On whose fresh lips basest falsehood dances.
And yet how dear to my heart was she!
And dear as ever she still must be.

My wife I've called her since in the wildwood.
We played together in happy childhood.
Of high achievement if e'er I thought,
Her love alone was the prize I sought;
As stems which grow from one root together,
If Thor strikes one then they both will wither;
If one its vesture of emerald shows,
The other mantles with green its boughs.
Our lives in joy and in grief thus blended,
I cannot think of the union ended.
But I'm alone. O, thou noble Var
Who wanderest over the earth afar,
To record on gold every vow that's spoken,
Forego thy pastime, the vows are broken.
The tablet filled with but falsest lies,
The faithful gold 'gainst the insult cries.
Of Balder's Nanna I've oft been dreaming,
But truth in mortals is only seeming.
In faithfulness can no heart rejoice
Since falsehood borrows my Ingeborg's voice,--
A voice like wind which o'er flower fields strayeth
Or harp-strings' music when Brage playeth.
I'll list no more when the harp is tried,
I will not think of my faithless bride;
Where storms are raging there will I follow,
Till blood thou drinkest, thou ocean billow.
Where swords sow seeds for pale death to reap,
On mount or vale I my vigil keep.
If king I meet and to combat dare him
I smile to think how my sword shall spare him.
But if in battle a youth I meet,
With heart enamored and visions sweet,
Deluded fool who on faith relieth,

I'll hew him down e'er the vision flyeth,
Will kindly slay him ere yet he be
Deceived, disgraced and betrayed like me."

"The blood that's youthful no boundaries heedeth,"
Old Hilding said, "how much it needeth
The cooling touch of the snows of age.
You wrong the maid with your senseless rage.
My foster-daughter beware of blaming
For adverse fortune which, heaven ordaining,
The wrathful norns upon men below
Hurl down, for none can escape the blow.
Like silent Vidar, no outward token
The maiden gave that her heart was broken.
Her grief was mute as in southern grove
The voiceless woe of the widowed dove.
To me alone who her childhood guided
Was all the pain she endured confided.
As dives the sea-fowl with wounded breast
Lest daylight's eye should upon it rest,
And there remaineth with life-blood flowing,
No sign of weakness or misery showing,
So she in darkness her suffering bore,
And only I saw her anguish sore.
She often said: 'I am but an offering
For Bele's kingdom; who talks of suffering!
The snow-drop fragrant, with leaf and vine
To deck the victim in wreaths they twine.
How sweet to die and escape from anguish!
But no, in pain must I live and languish;
For Balder's wrath will no rest allow

My aching heart and my throbbing brow.
But tell to no one my secret sorrow,
I'd rather suffer than pity borrow;
King Bele's daughter her fate may dare,--
But kindly greeting to Fridthjof bear.'
The wedding day with its footsteps fateful
Arrived at last. O, the day most hateful!
To the temple marched in procession sad,
The white-robed virgins and men steel-clad;
A bard dejected the train was guiding,
The pale bride followed, a black steed riding
As pale was she as the wraith which sits
On a storm-cloud black, when the lightning flits.
From off the saddle I quietly took her,
Nor at the temple door forsook her;
But led her up to the altar, where
Her vows she uttered in accents clear.
She wept and prayed, on good Balder calling,
While down her cheeks were the tear-drops falling.
When Helge saw on her arm your band,
He tore it off with an angry hand;
On Balder's image now hangs the jewel.
My wrath burst forth at this act so cruel;
My sword was by me, I drew it forth,--
King Helge then was but little worth.
'Let be,' said Ing'borg, in accents broken,
'My brother might surely have spared this token;
How much one suffers ere death sets free,--
The Allfather judgeth 'twixt him and me.'"

"The Allfather judgeth," said Fridthjof slowly,
"I too would give him my judgment lowly.
Is't not now mid-summer, Balder's feast?

And in the temple the crowned priest,--
The king, who sold the maiden tender?
Ah! yes, my judgment I fain would render."

XIII.
BALDER'S FUNERAL PILE.

Midnight's sun on the mountain lay,
  Blood-red was its gleaming
It was not night nor was it day,
  But just between them seeming.

Balder's bale-fire, symbol bright,
  On sacred hearth was burning,--
Soon is quenched its wasted light,
  Hoder's reign returning.

Priests around the temple wall
  Burning brands were grasping;
Silver-bearded, old men all,--
  Their hard hands flint knives clasping.

The crowned king stands the altar near;
  Hark! the midnight soundeth,--
With clash of weapons, sharp and clear,
  The sacred grove resoundeth.

"Bjorn, stand fast by yonder door,
  No one must pass under,
Whosoe'er would cross the floor,
  Cleave his skull asunder."

Helge paled: he knew too well
 Whose that voice so ringing.
Forth stood Fridthjof; his fierce words fell
 Like autumn storm winds singing.

"Here's the ordered tribute; it came
 Safe through the tempest's rattle;
Take it; then here by Balder's flame,
 For life or death we'll battle.

"Shields behind us, our bosoms free.
 Fair the fight be reckoned;
As king, the first blow belongs to thee,
 Mind thou, mine's the second.

"Caught at last is the wily fox,
 Vain all thought of flying;
Think of her with the golden locks,
 Of Framness wasted lying."

Thus he spake, and the purse he'd brought,
 Forth he quickly drew it,
Careless of the mischief wrought,
 In Helge's face he threw it.

Darkness swam before the eyes
 Of asas' kinsman sainted;
Blood gushed forth, he could not rise,
 But near his altar fainted.

"With the gold you as tribute claim,
 Are you overpowered?

None shall Angervadil blame
 For felling such a coward.

"Silence, priests with altar-knives,
 Moonshine princes, quiet!
Else my sword may drink your lives;
 Thirsting 'tis to try it.

"Holy Balder, thy wrath forbear,
 Nor 'gainst me enrol it:
But the arm-ring which you wear,
 Yonder craven stole it.

"Not for thee did Volund old
 Work its fair dimensions;
The maiden wept, but the thief was bold;
 Away, such false pretensions."

Bravely drew he; together fast
 Arm and ring seemed growing;
Angered Balder, when loosed at last,
 Fell 'mid the embers glowing.

Hark! each flame, as it leaps on high,
 A golden tooth resembles;
Bjorn, all pale, stands the doorway nigh,
 Fridthjof, anxious, trembles.

"Open, Bjorn, let the people go,
 Bv watchmen unimpeded;
The temple burns; throw water, throw
 The ocean full, if needed."

Now a chain is knit to the strand,
 Not a link is missing;
Flies the billow from hand to hand
 Against the fire-brands hissing.

Fridthjof sits like the god of rain
 High o'er beam and water,
Gives to all his orders plain,
 Calm amid the slaughter.

Vain! the fire has the upper hand,
 Smoke-clouds dense are growing,
Gold falls first on the red-hot sand,
 Silver streams are flowing.

All is lost! to the half-burned hall
 A fire-red cock is clinging,
He sits and crows on the roof-peak tall,
 His loosened pinions swinging.

The wind-blown flame mounts the vaulted sky,
 Everything it levels,
Balder's grove is summer dry,
 The hungry fire-king revels.

Fiercely leaping from height to height
 Aiming yet still higher;
O, what wild and terrific light!
 Strong is Balder's pyre!

Hark, it crackles! the roots now burn,
 The tops are fiery showers;

Muspel's ruddy children spurn
 Man's mere human powers.

A fire-sea billows in Balder's grove,
 Strandless breaks and hisses,
The sun is up, but bay and cove
 Mirror flaming abysses.

Soon in smoldering ashes lay
 Grove and temple's adorning;
Sadly then Fridthjof turned away,--
 Wept in the light of morning.

XIV.
FRIDTHJOF GOES INTO EXILE

On deck at night
In summer bright,
Sat Fridthjof grieving;
Like billows heaving,
Now wrath, now grief,
In his heart was chief;
And shoreward turning
Saw fires still burning.

"Thou temple reek
Fly up and seek
High Valhal's towers;
The White God's powers
Call down on me
With wrath's decree.
And tell, swift bounding,
The vault resounding,
The temple burned
To dust is turned;
The imaged glory
But lives in story.
Quick burned the god
Like common wood.

The grove protected
Nor once neglected
Since men swords bore
Is now no more;
By fire the slaying
Not time's decaying.
Forget no word
Thou hast seen or heard,
In Balder's dwelling
The story telling,
Thou message cloud
Of gods the shroud.
Long live in story
King Helge's glory,
Who exiled me
From him and thee,
My father's nation.
We'll roam creation
Where blue is king,
Where wild waves sing.
Thou canst not rest thee
Ellide, haste thee;
Earth's farthest bound
We'll sail around.
Soon thou'lt be rocking,
The sea-foam mocking,
My dragon good;
A drop of blood
Will nothing hinder
As on we wander.

In fiercest storm
Art thou my home;--

The one I cherished
By Helge perished.
Thou art my North
My foster-earth,--
The other leaving
I wander grieving:
My bride caressed
In black robes dressed;
The one in lustre
I could not trust her.

Thou ocean free,
Unknown to thee
Is king oppressive,
Untrue, aggressive.
Thy king is he
Among the free
Who trembles never
How high soever,
With wrath oppressed,
Heaves thy white breast.
Blue fields are charming
And not alarming;
There heroes plow
With keel and bow,
And blood-rain showers
In oaken bowers.
The good steel blade
Is seed-corn made.
The fields bring yearly
Not honor merely,
But gold as well.
Oh, kindly swell,

Thou ocean billow!
Thee will I follow.
My father's grave
Calm waters lave
(How still he sleepeth
Where green grass creepeth).
Mine blue shall be,
Flecked like the sea;
Forever floating,
On tempest gloating,
And fathoms deep
Draw men to sleep;
To me thou'rt given
For life a haven;
My grave thou'lt be,
Thou ocean free."

Thus inly burning
Sang Fridthjof, turning
His prow so true
From seas he knew,
And slowly creeping
'Mid rocks still keeping
Their faithful ward
O'er shallow fjord.

But vengeance watcheth;
King Helge fetcheth
Ten dragons out.
Thh people shout,
With breath abated:
"The king is fated;
He offers fight,

We scorn his might;
Though heaven-descended,
His reign is ended;
From earth we know
He now must go,
The blood god-given
Now longs for heaven."

Scarce was it spoke
Ere keels of oak
By unseen power
Began to lower;
Then on and on
Are downward drawn
To Ran's safe keeping.
King Helge, leaping,
Is glad to swim
From the sinking stem.
And Bjorn, none blaming,
Laughed loud, exclaiming:
"Thou asa-blood,
The art was good;
No one detected,
Or e'en suspected,
I bored so quick,--
A worthy trick!
May waves enfold them
And Ran still hold them
As heretofore.
It grieves me sore
That Helge misses
False Ran's cold kisses."

In wrathful mood
King Helge stood
From death delivered;
His round bow quivered,
Though made of steel,
As toward the shoal
So hard he drew it,
Though scarce he knew it,
It clanging broke.
Then Fridthjof spoke,
His lance well aiming,
While loud exclaiming:
"A death-bird here,
Enchained I bear:
If once set; flying,
Then low is lying
Thy coward head.
By Loke led
Thy fear abuseth;
My lance, refuseth

A coward's blood;
It is too good
For food so craven;
Its worth be graven
On funeral stone,
But not upon
A name which beareth
The stain thine weareth.
One exploit brave
Sank 'neath the wave;
The next one failed thee,
Nor aught availed thee;

Thy bow rust broke,
Not thou. The stroke,
When I aspire,
Is set much higher,
As thou mayst see
'Tis far from thee."

His carved oar limber
Was fir-tree timber,--
A mast-fir tall,
From Gudbrand's dale.
Taking another,
With both together
He rowed amain;
Like arrowy cane
Or steel blade brilliant
Were the oars resilient.
The sun climbs up
The mountain slope,
The winds, advancing
From land, to dancing
In morning's light
The waves invite.
Where foam-crest swimmeth
Ellide skimmeth
On joyous wings;
But Fridthjof sings:

"Thou front of creation,
 Exalted North!
I have no station
 On thy green earth.
Thy lineage sharing

My pride doth swell,
Thou home of daring!
Farewall, farewell!

Farewell thou royal
  Valhalla-throne!
Thou night's-eye loyal,
  Midsummer sun!
Thou sky unclouded
  As hero's soul!
Thou vault star-crowded!
Farewell, farewell!

Ye mountain ranges
  Where honor dwells,
Creation's changes
  Your rune-face tells.
Ye lakes and highlands
  I knew so well,
Ye rocks and islands,
  Farewell, farewell!

Farewell ye grave-mounds
  Where the linden showers
Near azure wave bounds
  The dust of flowers!
But time revealeth
  And judgeth well
What earth concealeth;
  Farewell, farewell!

Farewell ye bowers,
Beneath whose shade

So many hours
By brooks I've played;
Ye friends of childhood
Ye meant me well,
I love your wildwood;
Farewell, farewell!

My love is cheated,
 My home is burned,
My shame completed,
 I'm exiled, spurned.
From land appealing
 To ocean's swell,
Life's joyous feeling,
 Farewell, farewell!

XV.
The VIKING CODE.

Now he floated around on the desolate sea, like a
  prey-seeking falcon he rode,
To the champions on board he gave justice and law;
  wilt thou hear now the sea-viking's code?

"Make no tent on thy ship, never sleep in a house, for
  a foe within doors you may view;
On his shield sleeps the viking; his sword in his hand,
  and his tent is the heavenly blue.

See how short is the shaft of the hammer of Thor, but
  an ell's length the sword blade of Frey;
'Tis enough, for your weapon will ne'er be too short if
  you dare near the enemy stay.

"When the storm rageth fierce, hoist the sail to the top,--
  O how merry the storm-king appears;
Let her drive! let her drive! better founder than strike,
  for who strikes is a slave to his fears.

"Never take on thy vessel the land-sheltered maid; were
  she Freyja herself she'd ensnare;

For the dimples she wears are but pitfalls for men, and
　a net is her free flowing hair.

"Wine is Allfather's drink, and the cup is allowed if you
　only can use it with sense;
He who falls on the land may arise,--who falls here he
　to Ran, the sleep-giving, goes hence.

"If a merchant sail by, you must shelter his ship, but
　the weak will not tribute withhold;
You are king of the waves, he a slave to his gains; and
　your steel is as good as his gold.

"Let your goods he divided by lot or by dice, how it
　falls you may never complain;
But the sea-king himself takes no part in the lots,--he
　considers the honor his gain.

"If a viking-ship come, there is grappling and strife,
　and the fight 'neath the shields will rejoice;
If you yield but a pace you are parted from us; 'tis the
　law, you may act by your choice.

"If you win, be content; he who praying for peace
　yields his sword, is no longer a foe;
"Prayer's a Valhalla-child, hear the suppliant voice; he's
　a coward who answereth no.

"Wounds are viking's reward, and the pride of the man
　on whose breast or whose forehead they stand;
Let them bleed on unbound till the close of the day, if
　you wish to be one of our band."

Thus his law was enrolled,--and his name, every day,
 through all foreign coasts grew renowned;
For his like was not seen on the blue-rolling sea, nor the
 valor his champions crowned.

Then he sat by the rudder and sullenly gazed in the
 depths of the blue rocking tide;
"Thou art deep; in thy depths thriveth peace, it may
 be, but it thriveth not here where we ride.

"Is the White God enraged? Let him take up his sword,
 I will fall if it thus is designed;
But he sits in the skies, and the thoughts he sends
 down which forever are clouding my mind."

When the conflict came on, then his spirit arose like an
 eagle refreshed for its flight;
And his brow it was clear, and his voice it rang high,--
 like the thunderer first in the fight.

So from conquest to conquest unbroken he went, and
 was safe o'er the high, foaming grave;

And he saw in the south many islands and rocks, till
 he came to the calm Grecian wave.

When he saw the green groves that stand out from the
 waves, and the temple before him uprose,
What he thought Freyja knows, and the poet knows too,
 and the lover, he knows, ah! he knows!

"Here we ought to have dwelt, here's the island and
 grove, here the fane as my father set forth.

It was here, it was here I invited my love, but the cruel
  one staid in the North.

"Surely peace has its home in those blissful green dales,--
  in the colonnades, memory's words;
Like the whisper of love are the murmuring founts, and
  a bride-song the voice of the birds.

"Where is Ingeborg now? Hath forgotten me quite for
  the gray-haired and withered old king?
I can never forget, but my life I would give, if one sight
  of my love it would bring.

"Now three years have passed by since the land I beheld
  where heroic achievement prevails;
Tower the honored mounts yet to the heavenly blue? is
  it green in my forefathers' dales?

"On the grave where my father is laid I once planted
  a tree; can it be it lives now?
And who cares for the weakling? Thou earth give it
  moisture, and dew, kindly heaven, give thou.

"But why linger I longer on far distant waves, taking
  tribute and striking men down?
For my soul but despises the glittering gold, and I've
  gained quite enough of renown.

"There's a flag on the mast and it points to the North,
  in the North is the land I hold dear;
I will follow the course of the heavenly winds, and back
  to the Northland I'll steer."

XVI.
FRIDTHJOF AND BJORN.

Bjorn, I am weary of riding the sea,
 Turbulent traps are the billowy fountains;
 Northland's firm earth and her long cherished mountains,
Wondrous attractions, are calling to me.
 Happy is he by his land unrejected,
No one denies him his father's green grave;
 Too long, alas, have I wandered dejected,
Outlawed, afloat on this wilderness wave.

BJORN.

Good is the sea, your complaining you squander,
 Freedom and joy on the sea flourish best;
 He never knoweth effeminate rest,
Who on the billows delighteth to wander.
 When I am old, to the green growing land
I too will cling, with the grass for my pillow;
 Now I will drink and will fight with free hand,
Now I'll enjoy my own sorrow-free billow.

FRIDTHJOF.

Now hath the ice indeed chased us to land,

Close round our keel are the stiffened waves dozing;
 Let me not waste the long winter reposing
Here among rocks on this desolate strand.
 Let me once more keep the Yule banquet olden,
Guest of king Ring and the bride of my choice;
 Let me once more see those waving locks golden,
Hear the sweet tones of that well-beloved voice.

BJORN.

Good! to king Ring it shall be my glad duty,
 Something to teach of a wronged viking's power;
 Fire we the palace at midnight's still hour,
Scorch the old graybeard and bear off the beauty.
 Or, being viking you may think it right
Honor to grant the old man by a duel:
 Challenge him out on the ice for a fight,--
Whatever you will, only waiting is cruel.

FRIDTHJOF.

Speak not of firebrands, to war give no thought,--
 Peace would I bear to the king, and not terror;
 Ring nor his partner committed the error--
Heavenly vengeance my punishment sought,
 Little of hope is now left worth the telling,
Only farewell would I take of my dear,--
 Final farewell. When the green buds are swelling,
Sooner it may be, you'll see Fridthjof here.

BJORN.

Fridthjof, 'tis time for your folly's abating;

Sigh and lament for a false woman's loss!
 Earth is, alas, but too full of such dross;
One may be lost, still a thousand are waiting.
 Say but the word, of such goods I will bring
Quickly a cargo,-- the Southland can spare them,
 Red as the rose, mild as lambs in the Spring;
Then we'll cast lots, or as brothers we'll share them.

FRIDTHJOF.

Bjorn, you're as frank and as joyous as Frey,
 Bold to wage war and with wisdom advising;
 Odin and Thor you ne'er think of despising,--
Freyja, the heavenly, you dare to gainsay.
 Let us not question her power supernal,
Rather beware lest we waken her ire;
 Once, though now slumbering, the sparkle eternal
Mortals and gods shall enkindle to fire.

BJORN.

Go not alone, lest return be prevented.

FRIDTHJOF.

 Singly I go not, my sword goes with me.

BJORN.

 Hagbert, remember, was hanged to a tree.

FRIDTHJOF.

Who can be taken, to hang has consented.

BJORN.

Fallest thou then, on thy murderer fell
Carve I the blood-eagle, vengeance bestowing.

FRIDTHJOF.

Needless, fond Bjorn, he'll not hear the cock crowing
Longer than I do. Farewell, fare thee well.

XVII.
FRIDTHJOF COMES TO KING RING.

King Ring in state was seated at Yule-time drinking mead.
And with him sat his consort, so white and rosy red;
They seemed like Spring and Autumn. when both together seen,--
The king was chilly Autumn, fresh Spring the fair young queen.

A man, unknown, there entered within the spacious hall,
From head to foot enveloped, a bear-skin covering all;
And though by staff supported, and bent with age and care,
He stood a head the taller than any champion there.

He chose for seat to rest him a bench beside the door,--
'Tis now the poor man's station, as 'twas in days of yore;
The courtiers all laughed loudly, with many a gibe and jest,
And with the finger pointed to him in bear-skin dressed.

The stranger's eyes flashed lightning which made his anger felt,
And quick a young man seizing with one hand, by the belt,
Both up and down he turned him; then ceased the gleeful din,
For all the rest were silent,--so you and I had been.

"What causes such an uproar? who dares disturb our peace?
Old man, come here and answer, and let the tumult cease;
Your name, your place, your errand; come, answer if you can."

Thus spake the angered monarch to the half-concealed
old man.

"You ask me many questions, I'll answer every one:
My name (I will not give it) belongs to me alone;
My birthplace was misfortune, my heritage is want,--
I hither came but lately from wolf so fierce and gaunt.

"In youth I rode a dragon upon the waters blue,
Its wings were stout, and gayly and safely too it flew;
But crippled now and frozen, it leaves the land no more,
And I, grown old and weary, burn salt upon the shore.

"I came to see thy wisdom, renowned so far and wide;
And when they met me rudely (for scorn I'll not abide),
One idiot by the girdle I grasped, and turned him round,
For that I beg your pardon,--though now he's safe and sound."

"Thy words are wisely chosen," said Ring, "I must agree;
The aged should be honored, come sit thee here by me;
Slip off these false disguises and let thy form appear,--
Disguise is foe to pleasure, and pleasure ruleth here."

The guest now loosed the bearskin,--it fell from off his head,
Where stood old age decrepit, each saw a youth instead,--
From off whose noble forehead, and round whose shoulders brave,
The light locks fell and floated in many a golden wave.

In azure velvet mantle, he then stood forth erect,
His belt a silver girdle with forest beasts bedecked,--
Embossed by cunning workman, each figure deftly traced,
And round and round the hero they each the other chased.

A massive golden circlet his sinewy arm displayed;
His battle-sword hung by him as though the lightning stayed;
A hero glance about him he cast from time to time,
And stood as Balder beauteous, as Asa-Thor sublime.

Surprised, the queen's cheeks quickly with changing color glow,
As northern lights so ruddy paint fields of driven snow;
As two twin water lilies, alarmed by tempest's swell,
Stand swinging on the billow, her bosom rose and fell.

The horn a shrill blast sounded, then silence reigned throughout;
The hour for vows was coming, and Frey's boar now they brought;
His mouth contained an apple, wreaths on his neck were laid,
His four knees bent beneath him upon a silver cade.

King Ring, his gray locks flowing, arose and straight-way now
The boar's head gently touching, he thus declared his vow:
"I swear to conquer Fridthjof, the champion in war,
So help me Frey and Odin, and. likewise mighty Thor."

Then with a smile defiant uprose the stranger tall,
A look of wrath heroic spread o'er his features all,--
He smote with sword the table till through the hall it rang;
And up from oaken benches the steel-clad warriors sprang.

"And now, sir king, please listen while I my vow shall tell,--
Young Fridthjof is my kinsman, and so I know him well;
'Gainst all the world I'll shield him, I give you here my word,
So help me now my norn, and likewise my good sword."

The king then laughed. "Right daring, methinks, your speech," said he,
"But in this Northland palace shall all fair words be free;
My queen, fill him a bumper of wine, the very best,--

I hope that through the winter he'll here remain our guest."

The queen then took the goblet, before her it was placed,--
A rare and costly jewel, which once the ure's head graced;
It stood on feet of silver, and on its golden bands
Were runes of high achievement, engraved by skillful hands.

With downcast eyes she reached him the goblet, brimming filled,--
But with a hand so trembling that wine thereon was spilled:
As evening's shades so ruddy upon the lilies glow,
So gleamed the drops of ruby on hand as white as snow.

The guest the horn accepted with reverential bow,--
Not two men could have drained it, as men are reckoned now,--
Without an instant's waiting the strong man, at a draught,
The lovely queen to honor, the brimming ruby quaffed.

The skald at table seated, his waiting harp brought forth,
And sang a heartfelt story of true love in the North,--
Of Hagbert and of Signe; and at the deep tones' peal
Each warrior's heart was melted, though clad his breast in steel.

He sang of Valhal's mansions, of heroes' blest reward,
Of ancient deeds of valor, on fields of wave and sward;
Then grasped each hand its sword-hilt, then flashed each eye intent,--
And quickly round the table the foaming mead-horn went.

And lively was the drinking within that royal hall,--
An honest Yule carousal engaged the champions all;
The sleep that followed after no care or anger stained;
But Ring, the aged monarch, with Ingeborg remained.

XVIII.
THE RIDE ON THE ICE.

King Ring to a banquet his queen would take,
The ice like a mirror o'erspread the lake.

"Go not on the ice," said the stranger bold,
"It may break, and the bath is too deep and cold."

"The king," answered Ring, "is not easily drowned,
Whoever is fearful let him go round."

The stranger was angered and sullen frowned,--
Then quickly his skates to his feet he bound.

The sledge-horse sets out, he is strong and free,--
His nostrils are flaming, so glad is he.

"Strike out," cried the monarch, "my charger good,
And show if you are of the Sleipner blood."

As swift as a storm on the sea his speed;
The prayers of the queen does the king not heed.

The stranger in mail on his skates is not still,
But passes them swiftly whenever he will.

He writes many runes on the ice besides,--
And over her name lovely Ingeborg rides.

They swiftly speed onward, the lake to span,
But under them lurketh the treacherous Ran.

Her silvery roof in a trice she breaks,
And catches the sled in the hole she makes.

The cheeks of the beautiful queen turn pale;
Then comes like a whirlwind the skater in mail.

He buries his skate in the ice, to clasp
The steed's flowing mane in his iron grasp.

With one single effort his arm the swings,
And charger and sled to the firm ice brings.

"That stroke," said Ring, "was a noble one,--
Not Fridthjof, the strong, could have better done."

So they all returned to the house of the king,--
The stranger remaining until the spring.

XIX.
FRIDTHJOF'S TEMPTATION.

Spring is coming, song-birds twitter, woods are leafing, smiles the sun;
Dancing downward, toward the ocean, see the loosened rivers run;
Glowing like the cheeks of Freyja, from the buds the roses ope,--
Hearts of men to life awaken, full of courage, love and hope.

Ho! the chase! the aged monarch with his queen will go to-day;
Now in crowds the court assembles, waiting in confused array,--
Bows are clanging, quivers rattling, steeds impatient paw the ground;
Hooded falcons, wildly shrieking, make the echoing hills resound.

See! the queen appears! Poor Fridthjof, do not thither cast your eye;
Sits she on her milk-white palfrey like a star in spring's clear sky,--
Half a Freyja, half a Rota,--lovelier far than either one,--
From her dainty hat of purple, plumes are waving in the sun.

Look not on those eyes so heavenly,--of those golden locks beware!

Oh! take care! that form is supple, full that bosom, oh! take care!
Look not where the rose and lily shifting hues alternate fling;
Listen not to those loved accents, sighing like the winds of spring.

Now the hunting troop is ready. Hark, through hills and valleys all
Sounds the horn, the falcon loosened straight ascends to Odin's hall;

Forest denizens in terror haste to seek their cavern-homes;
But, with spear outstretched before her, each valkyrie swiftly comes.

Aged Ring no longer follows where the eager hunter flies;
By his side alone rides Fridthjof, silent, grave, with downcast eyes.
Darkest thoughts, and full of anguish, stir within his sorrowing breast,
And wherever he may wander, haunting voices banish rest.

"Oh, the sea! why did I leave it? thus to my own peril blind!
Sorrow thrives not on the billow, scattered 'tis by every wind.
Broods the viking? danger cometh bidding him the lance prepare;
Vanish then all sad reflections, blinded by the weapon's glare.

"Here, a longing, past describing, flaps its wings about my brow,
And like one asleep and dreaming, to and fro I wander now;
Balder's precincts I remember, nor forget the oath she gave.
'Twas the gods, not she, who broke it,--gods relentless as the grave.

"For they hate the race of mortals, on their joy with anger look,
So to deck cold winter's bosom, they my tender rose-bud took;
What does Winter with my blossom? Can he understand its worth?
Nay, but bud and stem and leaflet, clothes in ice with frosty breath."

Thus bewailed he. Soon they came into a dark and lonesome dell,
Gloomy, crowded 'twixt two mountains; o'er it densest shadows fell.
Then the monarch halted, saying: "See how lovely, fresh and deep!
I am weary and would rest me, fain would have a moment's sleep."
"Sleep not here, for hard and chilly is the ground, O king, indeed:
Up, thy sleep will not refresh thee, let me back the monarch lead."

"Like the other gods, sleep cometh unexpected. Does my guest,"
Said the king with feeble accents, "grudge his host a moment's rest?"
Fridthjof then took off his mantle, and outspread it 'neath a tree;

And the king, in trusting friendship, laid his head on Fridthjof's knee;
Soon he slept as sleeps the hero after battle's rude alarms,
On his shield, or as an infant cradled in his mother's arms.

As he slumbers, hark! there singeth from a branch a coal-black bird;
"Hasten, Fridthjof, slay the gray-beard, free your mind by discord stirred;
Take the queen, she's thine by promise; thee the bridal kiss she gave,
Human eyes do not behold thee; deep and silent is the grave."

Fridthjof listens; hark! there singeth from a branch a snow-white bird:
"Though no human eye behold thee, Odin sees and hears each word;
Coward, wilt thou murder slumber? Slay an old defenceless man?
Win what else, the crown of heroes is not won by such a plan."

So sang both the birds, but Fridthjof, snatching up his battle-blade,
Flung it from him with a shudder, far into the gloomy glade.
Black-bird flew away to Nastrand, airily the other one,
Singing, sweetly as a harp-tone, straightway mounted toward the sun.

Suddenly the old man wakens. "Much that sleep was worth to me;
Guarded by a brave man's weapon, sleep is sweet beneath a tree.

Yet I do not see your weapon; where has fled the lightning's twin?
What has parted you who never in your lives have parted been?"

"Little matters it," said Fridthjof, "'tis not hard to find a sword;
Sharp its tongue, O king. and never speaks for peace a single word;
Haunted 'tis by evil spirit, black, from Niflheim it roams,
Sleep is here in danger from it, seeking silver locks it comes."

"I, O youth, have not been sleeping, but to prove you have I tried;
Man or sword a wise man testeth, ere in them he will confide.
You are Fridthjof; since you entered first my hall I've known you well;

Ring, though old, at once detected what his guest would fain conceal.

"Wherefore, thus into my dwelling, crept you nameless, in disguise?
Wherefore, but to cheat and rob me, and my bride bear off a prize?
Honor, Fridthjof, sits not nameless, hospitality's rude guest;
Bright its shield as sun at noonday, on its face all eyes may rest.

"Fame had told us of a Fridthjof, whom both men and gods revere;
Shields he cleft and temples wasted, bold and brave, without a fear.
Soon with war-shield, so I reasoned, he will come against my land;
And he came, but clad in tatters, beggar's staff within his hand.

"Wherefore now cast down your eyelids? Once, like you, I too was young;
From the first is life a struggle, and fresh youth its Berserk-gang.
Hardly pressed and tried it must be, that its onset triumph not;
I have proved you and forgiven. I have pitied and forgot.

"Now am I grown old and weary, in the grave shall rest me soon,
Therefore take O youth, my kingdom, take my queen, she is thine own;
Be my son, till then remaining still my guest as heretofore.
Swordless champion shall protect me and our feud exist no more."

"As a thief," said Fridthjof sadly, "came I not, O king, to thee;
Had I wished thy queen to capture, tell me, who had hindered me?
But my bride, though lost forever, wished I to behold once more;
Fool was I! anew I kindled flames which were half quenched before.

"In thy halls too long I've tarried; here I must no longer stay.
Gods unreconciled their anger rest upon me day by day;
Balder, with the light locks flowing, loveth all mankind but one;
Only I am now rejected; see, he hateth me alone}!

"Yes, l set on fire his temple. Fane-profaner call they me.
Children shriek when I am mentioned, joy and gladness from me flee;
Northland casteth out the lost one, and in anger cries--depart!
In my native land I'm outlawed, I am outlawed in my heart.

"I will seek for peace no longer on the earth, so green and sweet,
Trees no more their shade aford me, burns the ground beneath my feet.
Ingeborg I've lost forever; she, my bride, accepted Ring,
From my life the Sun has vanished, night and noonday darkness bring.

"Therefore hence to ocean's billow! Out, away my dragon good,
Bathe again thy pitch-black bosom in the briny boiling flood;
Wave in clouds thine inky pinions, let the sea a path prepare,
Fly as far as star can guide us, far as conquered billows bear.

"Let me hear the rolling thunder, let me hear the lightning's voice;
When it thunders all around me, Fridthjof's heart will then rejoice;

Clang of shields and rain of arrows! Let the sea the battle fill;
Purified, I'll then fall gladly, reconciled to heaven's will."

XX.
KING RING'S DEATH.

Golden mane flowing,
  Skinfaxe duteous
Draweth the spring sun more bright than before;
  Morning beams glowing
  Doubly as beauteous,
Sport in the hall;--there's a knock at the door.

  Though his heart grieveth,
    Enters the stranger;
Pale sits the king, while the queen's gentle breast
  Billow-like heaveth;
    Singeth the ranger
A song of departure, with sorrow oppressed.

  "Bathes now the billow
    Winged steed flying,
Sea-horse is longing to flee from the strand;
  Glad will he follow
    Him who is hieing
Far from his home and his well beloved land.

  "The arm-ring I give thee,
    Ing'borg, receive it.

Holiest memories with it remain.
 Ne'er let it leave thee:
  Fridthjof, believe me
Truly forgives. Thou'lt not see him again.

 "No more beholding
  The smoke's upward motion
Northland I'll see. Truly man is a slave;
 Fate is unyielding;
  Far on the ocean
There is my fatherland, there is my grave.

 "When in your roaming
  Stars the vault cover,
Go not with Ingeborg down to the strand;
 Lest in the gloaming
  You should discover
Fridthjof, the outlawed, cast up on the sand."

 "Sad is the hearing,"
  Ring said, replying,
"When a man moans like a weak maiden's sigh.
 Valhal is nearing,
  E'en now the sighing
Death song I hear. Every mortal must die.

 "No one can frighten,
  Or by complaining
Change the allotment the norns have set down;
 Sorrow thou'lt lighten
  O'er the land reigning,--
Take thou my queen, for my son guard the crown.

"True is it spoken,
  Loved and respected
Peaceful I've reigned, over mountain and vale;
  Yet have I broken
  Shields, unprotected,
Landward and seaward, without turning pale.

"Now shall the bleeding
  Geirs-odd relieve me,--
Dying in bed ill befits Northland's kings;
  Not worth my heeding,
  Death shall receive me,--
Life's pain is equal to that which death brings."

Then carved he rightly
  Letters all glowing,--
Death runes to Odin on arm and on chest;
  Shine now so brightly
  Blood-drops o'erflowing,
Dyeing the silvery hair on his breast.

"Bring for my drinking
  The horn with wine flowing;
Skoal to thy honor, thou land of my birth!
  Minds deeply thinking,
  Harvest fields growing,--
Peaceful exploits have I loved on the earth.

"Vain amid slaughter
  Bloody and daring,
Sought I for peace,--she fled in dismay.
  Now the mild daughter
  Of heaven appearing,

Beckons me hence to Valhal away.

"Hail ye immortals!
  Sons of high heaven!
Earth disappears; Gjallarhorn to a feast
  Opens the portals;
  By the gods given,
Blessedness crowns as a helmet the guest!"

  Speaking intently,
  Ing'borg's hand loyal,
Also his son's, and his friend's, too, he pressed;
  Eyelids close gently,--
  Spirit so royal
Flies with a sigh to the Allfather's breast.

XXI.
RING'S DRAPA.

Sepultured sits he,
Sovereign descended,
Battle sword by him,
Buckler on arm;
Chafes his good charger
Champing impatient,
Pawing with gold-hoof
The gate of the grave.

Ring, great in riches,
Rideth o'er Bifrost;
Bends with its burden,
Bridge of the gods.
Wide for his welcome
Valhal it opens,
Hands to the hero
Heaven extends.

Absent is Asa-Thor,
Active in warfare.
Beckoned by Odin
The beaker is brought;
Frey the king graces
With garlands of grain-ears,

Blossoms the bluest
Binds Frigg therein.

Graspeth the gold-string,
Gray-bearded Brage,
Stiller now sigheth
The song than before;
Freyja the faithful,
Fondly reclining.
Bends o'er the board and
Burneth to hear.

"Sing high the smiting
Of sword upon helmet,
Boisterous billows,
Bloody for aye;
Power, the gift of
Gods ever gracious,
Bitter as berserk
Biting the shield.

"Hence was the hero-king,
Heaven-born dear to us,
Showing his shield
A shelter for peace.
Power's embodiment
Plainly impersonate,
Soared like a sacrifice-
Smoke to the sky.

"Words full of wisdom
Wise Odin chooseth
Sitting with Saga

Sokvabek's maid.
Such, too, the saying
Spoke by the monarch,
Fair as of Mimer
Flows the clear fount.

"Forsete faithful
All feuds adjusteth,
Sitting serenely
By the side of Urd's spring;
Thus high enthroned
Thou, king beloved,
Potently pleadest
For peace in the land.

"Niggard in nothing,
Near and far strewed he
Beauty and blessing,
Bought with his gold;
Gave he most gladly
Guerdon unstinted,
Sadness he solaced,
Suffering relieved.

"Welcome, thou wisest
Winner of Valhal!
Long thou'lt be lauded,
Loved of the North.
Brage, the bearded,
Bears thee the mead-horn,
Favored of fortune,
Friend from below."

XXII.
THE KING'S ELECTION.

"To thing! to thing!" from dale to hill
  The cry arose.
"King Ring is dead; his place to fill
  A king we'll choose."

From off the wall the peasant moves
  His steel sword blue;
Its edge his practiced finger proves,
  It biteth true.

The boys admire in pleased surprise
  The gleaming blue:
To lift the sword one vainly tries,
  It needeth two.

The daughter scours the helmet clean,
  Bright shall it be.
And blushes, in its silvery sheen
  Her face to see.

At last he takes his shield so round.
  A sun in blood;
"Hail! iron man, so strong and sound,
  Thou peasant good!

Renown and power which nations wield
 From thee they draw,
In war thou art thy country's shield,
 In peace its law."

The assembly met, while sounding high
 Were arms and shields,
In open thing, 'neath heaven's sky,
 In fair green fields.

Upon the thing-stone Fridthjof stands,
 And with him there
A little one with shining bands
 Of golden hair.

Then rose the cry on every hand:
 "Too small indeed
The king's son is to rule our land,
 Our wars to lead."

But Fridthjof on his shield raised up
 The little boy:
"Ye Norsemen, here behold your hope,
 Your king, your joy.

"High Odin's race embodied here
 In image see,
As much at home 'mid shield and spear,
 As fish in sea.

"I swear my lance and sword to set
 Round land and throne,

And with the father's coronet
To crown the son.

"The oath I make to Balder's son[4]
 Of high renown,
And if I fail, may he not shun
 To strike me down."

The boy sat on the shield so high
 As 'twere a throne~
Undaunted as the eaglet's eye
 Looks toward the sun.

At last impatient grew his blood,
 And to the ground,
The child leaped down and fearless stood ;--
A kingly bound!

Then rose the cry from all the thing:
 "We of the North,
We choose but thee, be like king Ring,
 Thou shield-borne youth.

"And Fridthjof shall a guardian be,
 Thy youth to guide;
His mother, earl, we give to thee,
 To be thy bride."

But Fridthjof frowned: "To-day," said he,
 "Election make,

---

4 Forsete

But not a bridal; leave to me
  A bride to take.

"To Balder's temple I'll repair,
  I go to see
The norns who are already there
  Awaiting me.

"With them a council I have willed,
  The shield-maids true,--
Beneath the tree of time they build,
  Above it too.

"Against me Balder's anger sore
  Doth still abide;
He took, he only can restore
  My cherished bride."

Saluting then the monarch new,
  He kissed his brow.
And o'er the broom-heath passed from view,
  Silent and slow.

XXIII.
FRIDTIMOF AT HIS FATHER'S GRAVE.

"How brightly smiles the sun, so friendly seeming.
 As swift from branch to branch its soft rays glide!
Allfather's light within the dew-drop gleaming,
 Is clear and pure as in the ocean wide.
See! all the mountain tops with red are streaming,--
 From Balder's altar flows the bloody tide;
In night will shortly sink the world's commotion,
As sinks the golden shield beneath the ocean.

"Yet let me first behold those well known places,
 My childhood friends that I have loved so well;
The same sweet beauty still the valley graces,
 The same birds yet alight in wood and dell;
The same blue wave the stable rock embraces,--
 Oh, would I ne'er had tried its treacherous swell!
It always speaks of fame and high endeavor,
But far from home it bears thee on forever.

"I know thee, stream, whose waters erst were freighted
 With swimmer bold, who with thy billows fought!
I know thee, too, thou vale where oft we plighted
 Eternal faith! Alas! earth holds it not!
Ye birchen trees, whose bark I carved delighted

With many runes, still wedded to the spot
Your white stems stand, crown-capped with sunshine golden,
All save myself unchanged since days now olden.

"Is all unchanged? Where, then, is Framness' dwelling,
 And Balder's temple on the sacred shore?
At thought of childhood's dales my heart is swelling.
 But fire and sword devoured them, they're no more.
Of human vengeance, of God's wrath their telling
 To wanderers over blackened field and floor;
Thou pious pilgrim, come not here to ponder,
For forest beasts in Balder's grove now wander.

"With Nidhug's curse each human life is teeming,--
 The cruel tempter from the land of shade,
He hates the asa-light with glory beaming
 On hero's brow and on his shining blade;
Each coward deed, each act of wrathful scenting,
 Is his, a tribute unto darkness paid;
He wins when temples burn and gods are slighted,
He claps his coal-black hands and laughs delighted.

"Is there no expiation, radiant heaven?
 Thou blue-eyed god, dost thou no penance take?
Man pardons man who has for pardon striven.
 When men atone the gods their wrath forsake;
By thee, the mildest one, I'm unforgiven ;--
 Command, and any sacrifice I'll make;
No will had Fridthjof in the temple's burning;
Oh! stainless make his shield, thine anger turning.

"Thy burden take away, I cannot bear it,
 The dark wood's music in my soul doth cry.

A moment's fault! cannot a life repair it,--
 An upright life? Then hear my contrite sigh!
If Thor's fierce bolt should strike, I still would dare it:
 Nor shrink to meet the look of Hel's pale eye.
Thou pious god, who moonlight glances bendest,
'Tis thee I fear, and vengeance which thou sendest.

"My father's grave is here. The hero sleepeth;--
 Alas! whence he has gone none ever roam;
A starry tent his home, no more he weepeth,
 Where shields rejoice and brimming mead-horns foam;
Thou asa-guest, from heaven look down where keepeth
 His weary watch thy child. O father, come!
I bring not runes nor charms, but bending lowly
Would learn to appease pale Balder holy.

"Still silent is the grave? Ah yes, and cruel.
 A sword roused Angantyr within his grave;
A sword is naught,--Tirfing a trifling jewel
 Compared with what I ask. A sword the brave
Can gain on battle field or in a duel,
 Forgiveness from the asas' home I crave;
Bear thou my plea, my sorrowing look to heaven,
No rest have noble minds if unforgiven.

"Thou'rt silent, father! Hear the waves resounding,
 And send thy loving word by their sweet cry;
Now flies the storm, on its swift pinions bounding.
 O, whisper to me as it flieth by;
See golden rings the western sky surrounding,
 Let them the message give which words deny.
No sign or answer for thy son forsaken?
How poor indeed are those whom death has taken!"

The sun is quenched. The evening breeze is stealing
 Upon earth's children with its lullaby,
And sunset tints in myriad circles wheeling
 Around the brim of heaven's rosy sky,
O'er hill and dale their azure hues revealing,
 A vision now of Valhal passeth by;
Then unexpected comes with rustling motion,
An image, gold and flames from western ocean.

A wondrous Hagring now the heavens covers.
 (The name that Valhal gives hath lovelier sound),
And over Balder's grove it gently hovers.
 A golden chaplet set in emerald ground;
Resplendence everywhere the eye discovers,
 Such lustre mortals ne'er before had found.
It stops and sinks to earth, not disappearing,
But where the temple stood, a temple rearing.

An imaged Breidablik its wall upreareth,
 (So burnished silver on the cliff had shone),
Each pillar cut of deep blue steel appealeth,
 The altar is a single precious stone,
A power unseen the vaulted roof upbeareth,
 A winter sky with sparkling stars o'erstrewn;
And there with golden crowns and robes befitting,
Of azure splendor. Valhal's gods are sitting.

With rune-writ shields, the maids of fateful power,
 The noble norns, within the portal stand,--
Three rosebuds springing in a single flower,
 A grave and yet a fascinating band;
While Urd is pointing to the ruined tower,--

The new one Skuld doth greet with welcome hand;
But scarce restored is Fridthjof, filled with blended
Delight and wonder, ere the scene is ended.

"From you, Time's maidens, comes illumination,--
 Thine, hero-father, is the token good:
The wasted shrine I'll build on sure foundation,
 In beauty shall it stand where erst it stood;
How excellent to thus make expiation,
 By peaceful deeds to atone for actions rude!
The outcast still may hope who sues in meekness,--
The White God softens, and forgives his weakness.

"All hail, ye myriad stars in splendor beaming!
 With joy I watch you silent tread the skies;
And welcome, Northern-lights. above me streaming,--
 No more a flaming temple to mine eyes:
Grow green, O grave! and from the wave bright gleaming,
 Thou wondrous melody again arise.

I'll sleep upon my shield, and dream how heaven
Forgets the faults its mercy hath forgiven.

XXIV.
THE RECONCILIATION.

Completed now was Balder's temple. Not enclosed
As heretofore with fence of wood; of hammered steel,
With golden knobs upon each bar, was built the fence
Round Balder's ground. Like steel-clad champions ranged for war,
With halberds and with golden helms, there stood it now
On guard around the sanctuary of the god.
Of giant stones alone the massive wall was built,
And joined with active skill, a noble giant work
For all eternity (as is Upsala's shrine,)
Where Norseland saw its Valhal in an earthly mold.
It stood there in its grandeur on the mountain cliff,
And mirrored in the ocean wave its lofty brow,
While round about it, like a zone of beauteous flowers,
Far stretched the dale of Balder with its sighing groves.
Its song of birds, a home where peace might reign supreme.
High rose the copper-bolted portal, and within
Two colonnades supported on strong omoplates
The vaulted canopy, and beautiful it hung
Above the temple, like a concave shield of gold.
At farthest end stood Balder's altar. It was hewn
From one huge block of northern granite: round it coiled
A graven serpent, covered o'er with written runes, -
Profoundest thoughts from Vala and from Ha'vama'l;

But in the wall above was left an open space,--
A dark blue ground all filled with golden stars; and there
A silver image sat--the pious god--as calm
And mild as sits the silver moon in heaven's blue.
Thus seemed the finished shrine. In couples entered now
Twelve temple virgins, clad in robes of silver gauze,
With roses glowing on their cheeks, and roses in
Their guileless hearts. Before the image of the god,
Around the altar newly consecrate they danced,
As light spring winds above the flowing fountains flit,
As dance the forest elves amid the waving grass.
While yet the morning dew. like pearls, lies glittering there.
And while they danced they joyful sang a sacred song
Of pious Balder, and how dearly he was loved
By every being; how he fell 'neath Hoder's dart,
And earth and sea and heaven wept. Yet sounded not
The song as though 'twere uttered by a human voice,
But as a tone from Breidablik, from Balder's home;
Or like the thought of lover to a lonely maid
When pipes the quail his deep notes in the hush of night,
And over northern birches falls the moonlight soft.
Enraptured Fridthjof stood; he leaned upon his sword,
And gazed upon the dance. Sweet childhood's memories thronged
His vision by,--an innocent and pleasant folk,
With smiling eyes reflecting heaven's blue, with heads
Surrounded hy a halo of bright locks, they waved
A kindly salutation to their childhood's friend.
Then sank the bloody shadow of his viking life,
With all its conflicts, all its perilous exploits,
Down into night, and in his fancy stood he forth
A flower-crowned monument above their grave.
And ever, as the song increased, his spirit soared
From earthly dales below to Valaskjalf above;

Then melted human hate and human vengeance, too,
As melts the icy coat of mail from off the cliff,
When shines the sun in spring. A sea of quiet peace.
Of silent ecstasy, possessed his hero-soul;
It was as if he felt the heart of nature beat
Against his own; as if, deep moved, he fain would fold
Creation in his brotherly embrace, and be at peace
With every living creature seen of God.
Then came into the temple Balder's priest most high,
Not young and beauteous as the god, but tall in form,
With heavenly mildness beaming in his noble face,
While down about his girdle flowed his silver beard.
An unused reverence possessed proud Fridthjof's heart;
The eagle wings upon his helmet meekly drooped
Before the aged man, who thus spoke words of peace:
"Son Fridthjof, welcome hither I've expected thee;
The strong man gladly roves around the earth and sea,
A berserk-like, who pallid bites the shield's hard edge,
But weary grown, and thoughtful, wanders home at last.
The powerful Thor went many times to Jotunheim,--
But spite his belt divine and gloves of finest steel,
Still sits the Utgard-Loke on his lofty throne;
For evil is itself a power, and will not yield,---
And piety not joined with power is children's play:
'Tis like the sunbeams on the breast of AEger thrown,--
An image faint, which falls and rises with the wave,
Foundationless and insecure, devoid of trust.
But power not joined with virtue eats itself away,
As rust the buried sword. 'Tis life's unchecked carouse;
The heron of oblivion hovers o'er the cup,
And when the drinker wakes, he blushes for his deed.
All power is from the earth of Ymer's body formed;
Wild waves and flowing waters are the veins therein,

From various metals are its tough strong sinews forged,
And yet 'tis empty, desolate, unfruitful, till
The sun its light and warmth, heaven's piety, sends down.
Then spring the grass and flowers a web of many hues;
The tree lifts up its crown and knits its golden fruit,--
And man and beast are nourished at the mother's breast.
'Tis thus with every child of Ask. Opposing weights
Has Odin laid within the scales of human life,--
And when they balance true, then even stands the beam;
And heavenly piety and earthly power they're called.
The power of Thor is great whene'er about his loins,
Immovable, he girds the belt of strength and strikes.
Indeed is Odin wise, when Urd's clear silver fount
He looketh down, and birds swift flying come to bring
The Asas' father tidings from the world's extreme:
Yet both turned pale, the radiance of their starry crowns
Was half extinguished when the pious Balder fell,--
The band was he of all the diadems of heaven.
Then withered on the tree of time its splendid crown,
And Nidhug gnawed upon its root; then were loosed
The powers of aged night. The Midgard serpent flung
Toward heaven its poison-swollen tail, and Fenris howled,
And Surt's swift fire-sword flashing gleamed from Muspelheim.
Since then wherever thou mayest look the strife goes on,
A war throughout creation. In Valhal crows
The cock with golden comb. Upon and 'neath the earth
The blood-red cock to battle calls. There once was peace
Not only where gods dwell, but also on the earth;
In man's as in the high gods' thoughts was peace.
Whate'er has happened here below has also chanced
In greater measure there; humanity is but
An image frail of heaven; it is as Valhal's light
Reflected in the shield of Saga writ with runes.

Its Balder hath each heart. Remember'st thou the time
When dwelt within thy breast sweet peace a guest, and life
As joyful seemed, as heavenly calm, as song bird's dream
When summer night-winds to and fro so gently wave
Each fragrant blossom sleeping in its bed of green?
Then holy Balder still abode in thy pure soul,
Thou asa-son, thou wandering image of high heaven.
For childhood Balder is not dead, and Hela gives
Again her prey us often as a child is born.
With Balder also groweth up in every soul
His brother Hoder, blind, the child of night; for blind
At birth is evil always, like the young of bears, and night
Its mantle, but the good of earth rejoice in light.
The tempter, busy Loke, always ready stands
To guide the blind one's murderous hand. The missile oft
To Valhal's love is sent, to Balder's tender breast.
Then Hate awakes and Violence upon its prey
Springs forth; the hungry sword-wolf prowls o'er hill and dale.
And fiercest dragons wild swim o'er the bloody waves.
For this meek Piety a powerless shadow sits
One dead among the dead, and with him pallid Hel,
And in its ashes Baldur's sanctuary lies.
So too the asa's life on high prefigures that
Mere human life below, and both are but the thoughts,
The silent thoughts of Odin which can never change.
What hath been, what shall be, that the song profound
Of Vala knows,--Time's lullaby, its drapa too.
Creation's annals have a melody the sam.
And man may hear his own life's history therein.
Dost comprehend or not? 'Tis Vala asketh thee.
Thou seek'st atonement; know'st thou what atonement is?
Oh, Fridthjof, look me in the eye and turn not pale!
Round earth a mediator goes, his name is Death.

A spark translucent, from eternity, is time:
All earthly life is but the refuse from Allfather's throne;
Atonement is to there return all purified.
The lofty asas fall themselves, and Ragnarok
The day of their atonement is, a bloody day
On Vigrid's hundred miles of plain; there will they fall,
But fall not unavenged, for there the evil die
Forever, but the fallen good arise again,
Refined, from out the flaming pyre to higher life.
'Tis true the star-crown, pale and withered, falleth down
From heaven's temple; earth too, sinks beneath the sea,
But brighter is it born again, and joyous lifts
Its flower crowned head from out the seething waves,--
And new created stars pursue with god-like glance
Their silent pathway round about the new-born earth.
But on the green hill-slopes will Balder govern then
The new-born asas, and a human race renewed.
The golden tablets filled with runes, lost long ago,
In Time's fresh morning, then are found amid the grass
On Ida's plain, by Valhal's children reconciled.
The fallen good in death are only tried by fire;
It is atonement made, a birth to higher life,
Which, purified, flies back to him from whom it came,
And plays a guileless child upon its father's knee.
Alas! that all the best is found beyond the grave,--
That gate of green which Gimle opens; vile is all,
Contaminated all that dwells beneath the stars.
And yet there is atonement found in life itself,--
A humble prelude to the peace of heaven above.
'Tis like the broken chords the minstrel strikes upon
The harp, when he with skillful fingers wakes the song;
The tone attuning with a gentle hand, before
With firmer touch he grasps the golden strings,--

Grand memories of old alluring from their grave,
While Valhal's splendor streameth on enraptured eyes.
For earth, indeed, is only heaven's shadow, life
The grounds in front of Balder's temple in the sky.
The people sacrifice unto the gods; the steed
Bedecked with gold and purple is an offering made.
A token this with meaning most profound,--for blood
Tints red the morning light of each atonement day.
But signs are not the substitute, they can not atone,
Thine own transgressions no one can amend for thee.
In Odin's breast divine the dead are reconciled;
Atonement for the living lies in their own hearts.
One offering, I know, unto the gods more dear
Than smoke of victims. 'Tis the sacrifice of thine
Own vengeance, and thy heart's untamed and bitter hate.
Canst thou not silence them, and canst thou not forgive,
O youth? What wilt thou then in Balder's sacred house?
With what intent hast thou this holy temple reared?
With stones is Balder not appeased. Atonement dwells
Below, as up above, alone where dwelleth peace.
With all thy foes and with thyself be reconciled.
The light-haired god will then be reconciled with thee.
They have a Balder in the south--the virgin's son,
Who by the Allfather wise was sent to explain the runes
Upon the norns' black shield rand,--unexplained before.
His battle-cry was peace, his conquering sword was love;
And blameless sat the dove upon his silver helm.
He holy lived and taught, he died and he forgave,--
And under distant palms his grave in sunlight lies.
From dale to dale his followers wander, it is said.
And melting hardened hearts, and laying hand in hand
Establish peace upon the reconciled earth.
I do not know the doctrine well, but dimly have I

In my better moments guessed what it may mean,--
And every human heart at times divines as well.
I know the time will come when it will lightly wave
Its white dove-pinions over all our northern hills;
But that day come, the North will be no more to us;
The oaks will sigh above our long-forgotten graves.
Oh, fortunate and blessed race! Ye who shall drink
The sparkling beaker of that light, I bid you hail!
It will be well if it can drive away the cloud
Whose humid covering hitherto has veiled life's sun.
But scorn not us, who, in sincerity, have sought
With unaverted gaze to find the light divine.
The Allfather is but one, though many herald him.

"Thou hatest Bele's sons. And wherefore hatest thou?
Because to thee, a yeoman's son, they did not choose
To give their sister, who belongs to Seming's race.--
The noble son of all-wise Odin. Their descent extends
To Valhal's throne,--and pride of birth is theirs.
Thou sayest that birth on fortune, not on worth, depends.
Of merit all his own, O youth, is no one proud,--
But only of his fortune; for the best of things
Are only God's good gifts to man. Art thou not proud
Of thy heroic deeds, of thy superior strength?
Who gave thee thy great strength? Did Asa-Thor not knit
Thy sinewy arms as firm and close as oaken boughs?
And is it not God's spirit high which joyous beats
Within the citadel of thine arched breast? Is not
The lightning God's which flashes in thy fiery eyes?
Beside thine infant cradle sang the haughty norns
The prince-song of thy life; for that thy merit is
No whit the greater than the king's son's for his birth.
Lest thy pride be condemned another's censure not.

King Helge now is fallen."
       Here broke Fridthjof in:
"King Helge fallen? When and where?"

       "Thou canst but know
That while thou here wert building, he was on the march
Among the Finnish mountains. On a lonely crag
There stood an ancient shrine. To Jumala 'twas built
Abandoned long ago,--the door was now fast closed;
But just above the portal still there stood a strange
Old image of the god, now tottering to its fall.
But no one dare approach, for there a saying rife
Among the people went from age to age, that he
Who first the temple sought should Jumala behold.
This Helge heard, and, blinded by his furious wrath,
Went up the ruined steps against the hated god,--
Intent to cast the temple down. When there arrived
The gate was closed,-- the key fast rusted in the lock.
Then grasping both the door-posts, hard and fierce he shook
The rotten pillars. All at once, with horrid crash,
Down fell the ponderous image, crushing in its fall
The Valhal-son. And thus he Jumala beheld.
A messenger last night arrived the tidings bore.
Now Halfdan sits alone on Bele's throne. To him
Thy hand extend, to heaven thy vengeance sacrifice.
That offering Balder asks, and I, his priest, require
In token that the peaceful god thou mockest not.
If thou refuse, this temple then is built in vain,
And vainly have I spoken."

       Then stepped Halfdan in,
Across the copper threshold, and with doubtful look
He stood aloof from him he feared and silence kept.

Then Fridthjof loosed the breastplate-hater from his side,
Against the altar placed his shield's bright golden orb,
And weaponless approached his silent waiting foe.
"In such a strife," said Fridthjof, in a kindly voice,
"The noblest he who offers first his hand for peace."
King Halfdan blushed, then off he drew his glove of steel,
And hands long separated met in friendly clasp,--
A hearty hand-shake, steadfast as the mountain's base.
And then the aged priest revoked the ban which on
The outlawed temple-violater long had lain.
'Twas scarce dissolved ere entered [Ingeborg, attired
In bridal robes and ermine mantle, with her maids,--
So glides the moon, whom stars attend, in heaven's vault;
With tear-drops in her lovely eyes, she fell upon
Her brother's neck; but he, with deep emotion, laid
His sister, grown more dear, on Fridthjof's faithful breast;
And o'er the altar of the god she gave her hand
To him, her childhood's early friend, her heart's beloved.

GLOSSARY.

For such explanations as are not found in the original notes we are chiefly indebted to Prof. R. B. Anderson, of the University of Wisconsin, and to his valuable work, NORSE MYTHOLOGY. We are also under obligations to Mrs. E. Hasselqvist, of the Augustana College of Rock Island, Illinois.

AEGER. The god of the stormy sea.

AEGER'S BOSOM. The sea.

ALFHEIM (elf-home). Frig's dwelling.

ANGANTYR. A champion who was slain in a duel hy Hjalmar the vigilant, and was buried with his sword Tirfing. His daughter Hervar called upon her dead father for the sword, and, according to the story, was answered. See Canto XXIII.

ANGERVADIL (grief-wader). Fridthjof's sword.

ASA. God. It is used as a prefix, as Asa-Thor, Asa-Loke. etc.

ASA-SONS. A people who came from Asia and. settled the North, and who claimed descent from the gods.

ASGARD. Home of the gods.

ASK. The first man.

ASTHILD. Cupid.

BALDER (the best). The mildest, the wisest and the most eloquent of the gods. He is the god of innocence, the White God. "Balder dies in nature when the woods are stripped of their foliage, when the flowers fade and the storms of winter howl. Balder dies in the spiritual world when the good are led away from the paths of virtue, when the soul becomes dark and gloomy, forgetting its heavenly origin. Balder returns in nature when the gentle winds of spring stir the air, when the nightingale's high note is heard in the heavens, and the flowers are unlocked to paint the laughing soil, when light takes the place of gloom and darkness. Balder returns in the spiritual world when the lost soul finds itself again, throws off tho mantle of darkness, and like the shining spirit soars on wings of light to heaven, to God who mgve it." See NORSE MYTHOLOGY, p. 294.

BAUTA-STONE. A rough stone set up at warriors' graves, and having no inscription.

BERSERK (bear-coat). The old Northern athletes or champions wore the skins of bears, wolves or reindeer, and went into battle with loud cries, wearing no armor.

BERSERK-GANG. The onset of the berserks.

BIFROST (the trembling way). The rainbow, the bridge of the gods.

BJORN (a bear). Notice the play upon this word in Canto X, p. 94: "Bjorn attend the rudder, Grip it with a bear's paw."

BLOOD-EAGLE. When a foe deserved especial cruelty, he was put to death by carving the picture of an eagle on his back. see Canto XVI, p. 150.

BRAGE. God of poesy: a son of Odin.

BRAN. Fridthjof's dog.

BREIDABLIK (broad-gleaming). Balder's abode.

BURN SALT. A common expression for making salt.

DELLING (day-spring). Dawn.

DELLING'S SON. Day.

DISARSAL. The temple of the goddesses.

DRAGON. A war vessel. See description of Ellide, Canto III, p. 30.

DRAPA. A funeral hymn, reciting the virtues of the deceased.

EFJE-SOUND. A sound in the Orkney Islands.

FAFNER. A son of Hreidmar and brother of Regin and Otter. Fafner and Regin demanded of their father a share of the gold obtained of Odin as Otter's ransom. Hreidmar refused, and Fafner slew his father, and, taking all the gold. assumed the form of a dragon and fled. He concealed tho gold on Gnita heath, where he was found by Sigurd, who, at the instigation of Regin, slew Fafner. He accomplished this by digging a pit in Fafner's path and concealing himself therein until the dragon passed over him, when he thrust his sword through Fafner's heart. See NORSE MYTHOLOGY, p. 377; also the story of the

Volsungs and Niblungs, translated by Magnusson and Morris. Sweden, 1870.

FAFNER'S BANE. The slayer of Fafner; Sigurd.

FENRIS. A wolf, and one of Loke's children. Chained by the gods until Ragnarok, he gets loose and conquers Odin, but is himself slain hy Vidar.

FOLKVANG (the folk-field). Freyja's dwelling.

FORSETE (the presider). Son of Balder and Nanna. The god of justice.

FOSTER-BROTHER. It was customary in the North, when two persons entered into friendship for life and death, or, as it was called, foster-brothership, that each wounded himself and allowed his blood to mingle with the other's. See, concerning Fridthjof and Bjorn, Canto III, p. 34.

FREY (a lord). The god of harvests: the dispenser of wealth.

FREYJA. Frey's soster, and goddess of love.

FRIGG. The wife of Odin and mother of Balder.

FUTHORC. The runes taken collectively are properly called the futhorc, the word being made up of the names of the first of the runes. Compare "alphabet".

GEFJUN. The goddess of maids.

GEIRS-ODD (spear-death). Death by the spear, self-inflicted. See Valhal.

GERD. Frey's wife, and very beautiful.

GIMLE. The heaven of heavens, where dwell the righteous after Ragnarok.

GJALLARHORN. The horn of Heimdal, the Saint Peter of the old mythology. It was heard all over the world.

GLITNER (the glittering). Forsete's golden dwelling.

GRONING-SOUND. A sound between the Danish Islands.

GUDBRAND'S DALE. Canto XIV, p. 138. in the diocese of Aggerhus, celebrated afterward (1612) for a battle in which the Norwegians slaughtered the forces of Col. St. Clair, the Scotch ally of Christian IV, of Denmark.

HAGBART. the sea-king, who became secretly betrothed to Signe, of Princess, thereby gaining the enmity of her father, who captured and hung him. Signe, unwilling to survive her betrothed, set fire to her dwelling and was burned to death.--See Cantos XVI and XVII.

HAGRING. Fata morgana.

HA'VAMA'L. The high song of Odin, containing many wise precepts for the government of men.

HEL. The goddess of death.

HILDER. The goddess of war.

HODER. The blind god; brother of Balder. Tempted by Loke, he slew Balder with the mistletoe.

IDA'S PLAIN. Where the gods assemble after Ragnarok.

IDUN. Wife of Brage. She is the rejuvenating goddess, the "ever-renovating spring," and hence she is dressed in green. --See Canto I, p. 5. She keeps the apples of immortality.

JOTUNHEIM. The abode of the Giants.

LOKE. The evil one. "He is the sly treacherous father of lies. In appearance he is beautiful and fair, but in his mind he is evil, and in his inclinations he is inconstant. Notwithstanding his being ranked among the gods, he is the slanderer of the gods, the grand contriver of deceit and fraud, the reproach of gods and men. Nobody renders him divine honors. He surpasses all mortals in the arts of perfidy and craft." -See NORSE MYTHOLOGY, page 373.

MIDGARD. The earth; the abode of man.

MIDGARD-SERPENT. A child of Loke. It was cast into the sea by Odin, and it grew till it reached around the whole world.

MIMER. The wise giant keeper of the holy well of wisdom.

MORVEN'S HILLS. Hills in the north of Scotland.

MUSPELHEIM. The abode of fire.

MUSPEL'S SONS. Flames.

NANNA. Balder's wife; goddess of flowers. She died heartbroken at Balder's death.

NASTRAND (the shore of corpses). Where the wicked are punished after Ragnarok.

NIDHUG. The dragon which lives in the fountain Hvergelmar and gnaws the root of Ygdrasil.

NIFLHEIM. The world of mists; the lower world; the place of punishment.

NORNS. The Fates. They are three: Urd, the past; Verdande, the present, and Skuld, the future. They control the destinies of gods and men.

ODER. Freyja's husband.

ODIN. The chief of the gods. He is the all-pervading spirit of the world, the governor of the universe, the author of war and the inventor of runes and of poetry. In appearance he is old, tall, one-eyed and long-bearded. He wears a broad-brimmed hat and a many-colored coat, and carries a spear called Gungner.

ODIN'S BIRDS. Odin has two ravens, Hugin and Munin (reflection and memory), which every day fly around the world and return to him with intelligence of all that happens.

PEASANT. The piece of lowest rank in chess; a pawn.

RAGNAROK (the twilight of the gods). The day of the destruction of the world, and of the regeneration of gods and men. See Canto XXIV.

RAN (the robber). Goddess of the sea; wife of AEger.

ROTA. One of Valhal's maidens; a valkyrie.

RUNES. The letters of the ancient Scandinavian alphabet were called runes (secrets). The runes were sixteen in number, and previous to the introduction of Christianity they were supposed to have been invented by Odin himself. A knowledge of them was for a long time confined to a few, who use them for the purposes of sorcery.

RUNE-STONE. A stone inscribed with runes, and set up at graves or elsewhere as a monument.

SAGA. Goddess of history; hence a history.

SEMING. A son of Odin. The early kings of Norway traced their lineage directly to Seming.

SIGNE. See Hagbart

SKINFAXE (shining mane). The horse of Day.

SKOAL. A health.

SKULD. The future. See Norns.

SLEIPNER (the slipper). Odin's course with eight feet.

SOKVABEK. Dwelling of Saga.

SURT. God of fire.

THING (pronounced ting). A deliberative assemblage of Norsemen, composed of all who were capable of bearing arms. It was held in the open air. The thingsmen expressed approval of any measure by striking the shield with the sword.

THOR. The second of the gods; the thunderer; the subduer of the frost giants.

He has a red beard; his weapon is a short-handled hammer called Mjolner. He is girt with a belt of strength, and wears iron gloves. His sons are Magne and Mode, strength and courage.

URD. The past. See Norns.

URD'S FOUNT. The fountain from which the norns sprinkled the tree Ygdrasil.

UTGARD-LOKE. The Loke of the Giants,--called Utgard, because he dwelt in the uttermost parts of the world, Jotunheim.

VALA. A prophetess.

VALASKJALF. Odin's dwelling.

VALHAL (the hall of the slain). Only those who fell by wounds received in battle, or self-inflicted, were entitled to the joys of Valhal, where they were feasted by Odin and attended by the valkyries.

VALKYRIES (choosers of the slain). Goddesses who serve in Valhal and go on Odin's errands.

VAR. The goddess who presides over marriages.

VEGTAM. A name assumed by Odin when he went to consult the vala concerning the fate of Balder.--See NORSE MYTHOLOGY, page 281.

VIDAR (forest). The silent god; a son of Odin. He slays the Fenris-wolf at Ragnarok.

VINGOLF (floor of friends). Freyja's dwelling.

VOLUND. A renowned smith corresponding to Vulcan.

YGDRASIL. An ash tree; the tree of the world. The norns sprinkled the top with water from Urd's fountain and thus kept it alive, although Nidhug gnawed its roots.

YMER. An enormous giant slain by the gods, and of whose body they created the world.

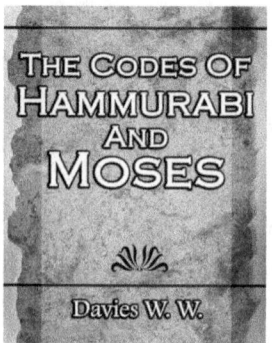

The Codes Of Hammurabi And Moses
W. W. Davies

QTY

The discovery of the Hammurabi Code is one of the greatest achievements of archaeology, and is of paramount interest, not only to the student of the Bible, but also to all those interested in ancient history...

Religion **ISBN:** *1-59462-338-4* Pages:132

MSRP $12.95

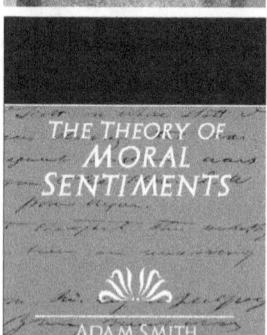

The Theory of Moral Sentiments
Adam Smith

QTY

This work from 1749. contains original theories of conscience amd moral judgment and it is the foundation for systemof morals.

Philosophy **ISBN:** *1-59462-777-0* Pages:536

MSRP $19.95

Jessica's First Prayer
Hesba Stretton

QTY

In a screened and secluded corner of one of the many railway-bridges which span the streets of London there could be seen a few years ago, from five o'clock every morning until half past eight, a tidily set-out coffee-stall, consisting of a trestle and board, upon which stood two large tin cans, with a small fire of charcoal burning under each so as to keep the coffee boiling during the early hours of the morning when the work-people were thronging into the city on their way to their daily toil...

Pages:84

Childrens **ISBN:** *1-59462-373-2* *MSRP $9.95*

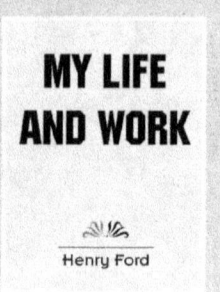

My Life and Work
Henry Ford

QTY

Henry Ford revolutionized the world with his implementation of mass production for the Model T automobile. Gain valuable business insight into his life and work with his own auto-biography... "We have only started on our development of our country we have not as yet, with all our talk of wonderful progress, done more than scratch the surface. The progress has been wonderful enough but..."

Pages:300

Biographies/ **ISBN:** *1-59462-198-5* *MSRP $21.95*

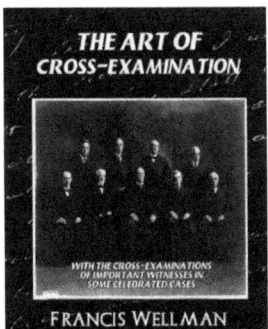

The Art of Cross-Examination
Francis Wellman

QTY

I presume it is the experience of every author, after his first book is published upon an important subject, to be almost overwhelmed with a wealth of ideas and illustrations which could readily have been included in his book, and which to his own mind, at least, seem to make a second edition inevitable. Such certainly was the case with me; and when the first edition had reached its sixth impression in five months, I rejoiced to learn that it seemed to my publishers that the book had met with a sufficiently favorable reception to justify a second and considerably enlarged edition. ..

Pages:412

Reference　　ISBN: *1-59462-647-2*　　*MSRP $19.95*

On the Duty of Civil Disobedience
Henry David Thoreau

QTY

Thoreau wrote his famous essay, On the Duty of Civil Disobedience, as a protest against an unjust but popular war and the immoral but popular institution of slave-owning. He did more than write—he declined to pay his taxes,   and was hauled off to gaol in consequence. Who can say how much this refusal of his hastened the end of the war and of slavery ?

Law　　　　ISBN: *1-59462-747-9*　　**Pages:48**

MSRP $7.45

Dream Psychology Psychoanalysis for Beginners
Sigmund Freud

QTY

Sigmund Freud, born Sigismund Schlomo Freud (May 6, 1856 - September 23, 1939), was a Jewish-Austrian neurologist and psychiatrist who co-founded the psychoanalytic school of psychology. Freud is best known for his theories of the unconscious mind, especially involving the mechanism of repression; his redefinition of sexual desire as mobile and directed towards a wide variety of objects; and his therapeutic techniques, especially his understanding of transference in the therapeutic relationship and the presumed value of dreams as sources of insight into unconscious desires.

Pages:196

Psychology　　ISBN: *1-59462-905-6*　　*MSRP $15.45*

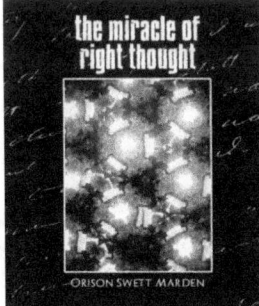

The Miracle of Right Thought
Orison Swett Marden

QTY

Believe with all of your heart that you will do what you were made to do. When the mind has once formed the habit of holding cheerful, happy, prosperous pictures, it will not be easy to form the opposite habit. It does not matter how improbable or how far away this realization may see, or how dark the prospects may be, if we visualize them as best we can, as vividly as possible, hold tenaciously to them and vigorously struggle to attain them, they will gradually become actualized, realized in the life. But a desire, a longing without endeavor, a yearning abandoned or held indifferently will vanish without realization.

Pages:360

Self Help　　　　ISBN: *1-59462-644-8*　　*MSRP $25.45*

QTY

The Rosicrucian Cosmo-Conception Mystic Christianity *by Max Heindel*
ISBN: *1-59462-188-8* **$38.95**
The Rosicrucian Cosmo-conception is not dogmatic, neither does it appeal to any other authority than the reason of the student. It is: not controversial, but is: sent forth in the, hope that it may help to clear...
New Age/Religion Pages 646

Abandonment To Divine Providence *by Jean-Pierre de Caussade*
ISBN: *1-59462-228-0* **$25.95**
"The Rev. Jean Pierre de Caussade was one of the most remarkable spiritual writers of the Society of Jesus in France in the 18th Century. His death took place at Toulouse in 1751. His works have gone through many editions and have been republished...
Inspirational/Religion Pages 400

Mental Chemistry *by Charles Haanel*
ISBN: *1-59462-192-6* **$23.95**
Mental Chemistry allows the change of material conditions by combining and appropriately utilizing the power of the mind. Much like applied chemistry creates something new and unique out of careful combinations of chemicals the mastery of mental chemistry...
New Age Pages 354

The Letters of Robert Browning and Elizabeth Barret Barrett 1845-1846 vol II
ISBN: *1-59462-193-4* **$35.95**
by Robert Browning and Elizabeth Barrett
Biographies Pages 596

Gleanings In Genesis (volume I) *by Arthur W. Pink*
ISBN: *1-59462-130-6* **$27.45**
Appropriately has Genesis been termed "the seed plot of the Bible" for in it we have, in germ form, almost all of the great doctrines which are afterwards fully developed in the books of Scripture which follow...
Religion/Inspirational Pages 420

The Master Key *by L. W. de Laurence*
ISBN: *1-59462-001-6* **$30.95**
In no branch of human knowledge has there been a more lively increase of the spirit of research during the past few years than in the study of Psychology, Concentration and Mental Discipline. The requests for authentic lessons in Thought Control, Mental Discipline and...
New Age/Business Pages 422

The Lesser Key Of Solomon Goetia *by L. W. de Laurence*
ISBN: *1-59462-092-X* **$9.95**
This translation of the first book of the "Lemegton" which is now for the first time made accessible to students of Talismanic Magic was done, after careful collation and edition, from numerous Ancient Manuscripts in Hebrew, Latin, and French...
New Age/Occult Pages 92

Rubaiyat Of Omar Khayyam *by Edward Fitzgerald*
ISBN:*1-59462-332-5* **$13.95**
Edward Fitzgerald, whom the world has already learned, in spite of his own efforts to remain within the shadow of anonymity, to look upon as one of the rarest poets of the century, was born at Bredfield, in Suffolk, on the 31st of March, 1809. He was the third son of John Purcell...
Music Pages 172

Ancient Law *by Henry Maine*
ISBN: *1-59462-128-4* **$29.95**
The chief object of the following pages is to indicate some of the earliest ideas of mankind, as they are reflected in Ancient Law, and to point out the relation of those ideas to modern thought.
Religion/History Pages 452

Far-Away Stories *by William J. Locke*
ISBN: *1-59462-129-2* **$19.45**
"Good wine needs no bush, but a collection of mixed vintages does. And this book is just such a collection. Some of the stories I do not want to remain buried for ever in the museum files of dead magazine-numbers an author's not unpardonable vanity..."
Fiction Pages 272

Life of David Crockett *by David Crockett*
ISBN: *1-59462-250-7* **$27.45**
"Colonel David Crockett was one of the most remarkable men of the times in which he lived. Born in humble life, but gifted with a strong will, an indomitable courage, and unremitting perseverance...
Biographies/New Age Pages 424

Lip-Reading *by Edward Nitchie*
ISBN: *1-59462-206-X* **$25.95**
Edward B. Nitchie, founder of the New York School for the Hard of Hearing, now the Nitchie School of Lip-Reading, Inc, wrote "LIP-READING Principles and Practice". The development and perfecting of this meritorious work on lip-reading was an undertaking...
How-to Pages 400

A Handbook of Suggestive Therapeutics, Applied Hypnotism, Psychic Science
ISBN: *1-59462-214-0* **$24.95**
by Henry Munro
Health/New Age/Health/Self-help Pages 376

A Doll's House: and Two Other Plays *by Henrik Ibsen*
ISBN: *1-59462-112-8* **$19.95**
Henrik Ibsen created this classic when in revolutionary 1848 Rome. Introducing some striking concepts in playwriting for the realist genre, this play has been studied the world over.
Fiction/Classics/Plays 308

The Light of Asia *by sir Edwin Arnold*
ISBN: *1-59462-204-3* **$13.95**
In this poetic masterpiece, Edwin Arnold describes the life and teachings of Buddha. The man who was to become known as Buddha to the world was born as Prince Gautama of India but he rejected the worldly riches and abandoned the reigns of power when...
Religion/History/Biographies Pages 170

The Complete Works of Guy de Maupassant *by Guy de Maupassant*
ISBN: *1-59462-157-8* **$16.95**
"For days and days, nights and nights, I had dreamed of that first kiss which was to consecrate our engagement, and I knew not on what spot I should put my lips..."
Fiction/Classics Pages 240

The Art of Cross-Examination *by Francis L. Wellman*
ISBN: *1-59462-309-0* **$26.95**
Written by a renowned trial lawyer, Wellman imparts his experience and uses case studies to explain how to use psychology to extract desired information through questioning.
How-to/Science/Reference Pages 408

Answered or Unanswered? *by Louisa Vaughan*
ISBN: *1-59462-248-5* **$10.95**
Miracles of Faith in China
Religion Pages 112

The Edinburgh Lectures on Mental Science (1909) *by Thomas*
ISBN: *1-59462-008-3* **$11.95**
This book contains the substance of a course of lectures recently given by the writer in the Queen Street Hall, Edinburgh. Its purpose is to indicate the Natural Principles governing the relation between Mental Action and Material Conditions...
New Age/Psychology Pages 148

Ayesha *by H. Rider Haggard*
ISBN: *1-59462-301-5* **$24.95**
Verily and indeed it is the unexpected that happens! Probably if there was one person upon the earth from whom the Editor of this, and of a certain previous history, did not expect to hear again...
Classics Pages 380

Ayala's Angel *by Anthony Trollope*
ISBN: *1-59462-352-X* **$29.95**
The two girls were both pretty, but Lucy who was twenty-one who supposed to be simple and comparatively unattractive, whereas Ayala was credited, as her Bombwhat romantic name might show, with poetic charm and a taste for romance. Ayala when her father died was nineteen...
Fiction Pages 484

The American Commonwealth *by James Bryce*
ISBN: *1-59462-286-8* **$34.45**
An interpretation of American democratic political theory. It examines political mechanics and society from the perspective of Scotsman James Bryce.
Politics Pages 572

Stories of the Pilgrims *by Margaret P. Pumphrey*
ISBN: *1-59462-116-0* **$17.95**
This book explores pilgrims religious oppression in England as well as their escape to Holland and eventual crossing to America on the Mayflower, and their early days in New England...
History Pages 268

QTY

The Fasting Cure *by Sinclair Upton* ISBN: *1-59462-222-1* **$13.95**
In the Cosmopolitan Magazine for May, 1910, and in the Contemporary Review (London) for April, 1910, I published an article dealing with my experiences in fasting. I have written a great many magazine articles, but never one which attracted so much attention... New Age/Self Help/Health Pages 164

Hebrew Astrology *by Sepharial* ISBN: *1-59462-308-2* **$13.45**
In these days of advanced thinking it is a matter of common observation that we have left many of the old landmarks behind and that we are now pressing forward to greater heights and to a wider horizon than that which represented the mind-content of our progenitors... Astrology Pages 144

Thought Vibration or The Law of Attraction in the Thought World ISBN: *1-59462-127-6* **$12.95**
by William Walker Atkinson Psychology/Religion Pages 144

Optimism *by Helen Keller* ISBN: *1-59462-108-X* **$15.95**
Helen Keller was blind, deaf, and mute since 19 months old, yet famously learned how to overcome these handicaps, communicate with the world, and spread her lectures promoting optimism. An inspiring read for everyone... Biographies/Inspirational Pages 84

Sara Crewe *by Frances Burnett* ISBN: *1-59462-360-0* **$9.45**
In the first place, Miss Minchin lived in London. Her home was a large, dull, tall one, in a large, dull square, where all the houses were alike, and all the sparrows were alike, and where all the door-knockers made the same heavy sound... Childrens/Classic Pages 88

The Autobiography of Benjamin Franklin *by Benjamin Franklin* ISBN: *1-59462-135-7* **$24.95**
The Autobiography of Benjamin Franklin has probably been more extensively read than any other American historical work, and no other book of its kind has had such ups and downs of fortune. Franklin lived for many years in England, where he was agent... Biographies/History Pages 332

Name	
Email	
Telephone	
Address	
City, State ZIP	

☐ **Credit Card**   ☐ **Check / Money Order**

Credit Card Number	
Expiration Date	
Signature	

Please Mail to: Book Jungle
PO Box 2226
Champaign, IL 61825
or Fax to: 630-214-0564

ORDERING INFORMATION

web: *www.bookjungle.com*
email: *sales@bookjungle.com*
fax: *630-214-0564*
mail: *Book Jungle PO Box 2226 Champaign, IL 61825*
or PayPal *to sales@bookjungle.com*

Please contact us for bulk discounts

DIRECT-ORDER TERMS

**20% Discount if You Order
Two or More Books**
Free Domestic Shipping!
Accepted: Master Card, Visa,
Discover, American Express